Praise for
Puro Pinche True Fictions

Puro Pinche True Fictions is a beautiful, poignant and affecting, highly original, inventive and innovative mixed-genre book, full of quiet wisdom, by turns bittersweet and delightfully humorous. An uplifting, luminous work, putting this reader in the mind of the late great Abkhazian-Russian writer Fazil Iskander's brilliant epic *Sandro of Chegem*.

— **Mikhail Iossel**, author of *Love Like Water, Love Like Fire*

From pop cultural musings to bloodcurdling family legends and pre-conquest lore, Alaniz folds time and space, inviting us to dip in. Serious and deeply probing as well as irreverent and rollicking fun, Alaniz joins our pantheon of greats like Oscar "Zeta" Acosta, Dagoberto Gilb, Michele Seros, Myriam Gurba, and José Antonio Burciaga. Roll that top back and fasten tight those lap belts, 'cause *Puro Pinche* is gonna take you for one heck of a ride.

— **Frederick Luis Aldama**, award-winning author and the Jacob & Frances Sanger Mossiker Chair in the Humanities at UT Austin

The stories, pictures, and memories woven by José Alaniz touch the reader like a caress from Mnemosyne or a chingazo from Tezcatlipoca. A hybrid book poised between prose fiction and comics, Alaniz's unique volume awakens readers to the mysteries and revelations of the Rio Grande Valley and worlds beyond.

— **Dr. William "Memo" Nericcio**, Curator of the Mextasy Circus of Desmadres and Professor, English and Comparative Literature, at San Diego State University

PURO PINCHE
TRUE FICTIONS

FLOWERSONG PRESS

Prose & Comics by

JOSÉ ALANIZ

FLOWERSONG
PRESS

FlowerSong Press
Copyright © 2023 by José Alaniz
ISBN: 978-1-953447-68-5

Published by FlowerSong Press
in the United States of America.
www.flowersongpress.com

Cover Art by José Alaniz
Cover Design by Edward Vidaurre
Set in Adobe Garamond Pro

NOTICE: SCHOOLS AND BUSINESSES
FlowerSong Press offers copies of this book at quantity discount with bulk
purchase for educational, business, or sales promotional use. For information,
please email the Publisher at info@flowersongpress.com.

This book was made possible by the generosity
of "Dr. Enrique E. Figueroa's GenteChicana/
SOYmosChicanos Arts Fund, which is a Donor
Advised Fund at the Greater Milwaukee Foundation".

para mi madre, Raquel Alaniz

Foreword

These stories in prose and comics form come from many different influences and parts of my life, though in one way or another they are all about growing up in the Rio Grande Valley, about my family, and about trying to leave.

Some of them are me channeling an alternate universe Ray Bradbury who had grown up Chicano.

These stories are also all in one way or another true and in one way or another made up.

Like all writing.

Thanks for taking the time.
Thanks also to my family and to Edward Vidaurre.

— **José Alaniz**
June 2023
Longbranch, WA

PURO PINCHE
TABLE OF CONTENTS

Genoveva 2010/1924......3

Sandías 1918......8

Tamales 2063......16

La Tormenta 1968......28

Solito 1972......33

The Bike 1978......39

Sam 1986......43

The Last Time 1994......53

Faccia Prima 1997......65

Dad Checks Out 20—......79

Where You Stop the Story 2022/1984......84

ELECTRIC YOUTH (COMICS)

Bzzzz!......95

Fragments......96

Fragments 2......97

El Otro Lado......98

Alone......99

Mordido......100

Una Cucharita De Azúcar......102

Burning Garage......103

El Ojo......104

Scary......105

Fruitful......106

One Time in Kindergarten (Me Cagué)......107

Brownie......108

Burning Basket......109

Banana Bike......110

Oh No!......111

The Nail......112

The Trunk......113

Not Proud of This One......114

Monte Cristo......115

Author Bio......117

PURO
PINCHE
TRUE FICTIONS

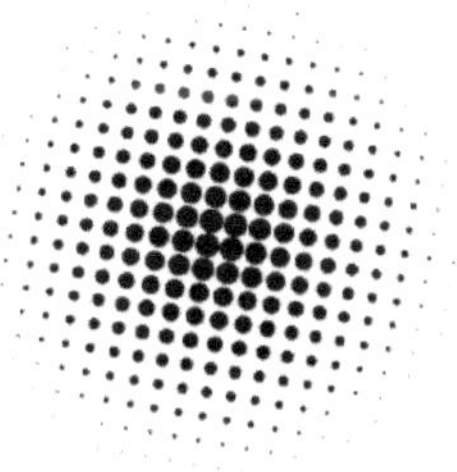

Genoveva

2010/1924

My paternal grandfather, Pedro Alaniz, died in September 2016, in his early 90s.

I of course remember a lot of things about him, not all of them good, but he was our patriarch, the longest-lived of all the abuelos.[1] We loved him, he died, ashes scattered, y ya, ya, ya.

That's more or less how he would have reacted. Ya se acabó el borlote. Wipe your hands and move on. In other words, he had an extremely dichotomous take on language. Something was either good or bad, all or nothing, here or far, far away. He loved the sweeping gesture, the binary world. His most-used palabras were "todo" and "nada": "¡Me lo tomo todo!" (though not in reference to alcohol; he had given up drinking and smoking long ago); "¡No quiero nada!"; "No hay problema"; "¡Tira toda esa basura! ¡Pa fuera!" Categorical, absolute, boom. Not much space for subtlety, or nuance. Todo o nada. El Jefe, el gallo, el más chingón. That was his kind of talk (minus the swearing).

He told stories that way, too, plenty of 'em. Things happened quickly in these cuentitos, effects swiftly followed causes – direct, unequivocal, sans appeal. Así es, y ya. He especially loved stories with a strong moral, where wrongdoers got what they deserved, even if such strained the bounds of proportion or human kindness. Justice above all.

Of course, in these cuentos justice mostly meant the righteous suffering

---

[1] In honor of his memory I have refrained from writing "abuelx" as I normally would, but to which he would likely have reacted with, "¿Qué es ese mugrero?"

of people who had wronged him. Like the one about when he and Grandma Concha were traveling up north, a long time ago, I think in Mississippi. They go into a restaurant for lunch. The manager walks up to their table and tells them they couldn't eat there. No Mexicans allowed. In such situations, Pedro (according to him) never objected, never made a scene; the very picture of wounded restraint. "We'll leave," he told the man, calmly, "but God is going to punish you for what you did."

A year later … by the way, a lot of "a year laters" and a lot of returns to the scene in my grandfather's stories – basically meaning time had passed (not necessarily, and probably not, an actual year) and now we would see a rightful balancing of the scales. I.e., enemies punished.

Anyway, "a year later," Grandma and Grandpa return to the same restaurant. Pedro spots the same man, the owner, in a wheelchair. He walks up to him and says, triumphantly, "You see? God punished you, just like I said he would." Colorín colorado, este cuento se ha acabado.

Another one. I heard him tell it twice to two different sets of people over the course of a long holiday dinner. An old friend had a drinking problem. Pedro got tired of seeing him drunk all the time, so one time he snatched his beer away from him. "¿Quien chingao eres tú, que me la quitas? ¡Dámela, pendejo!" Something like that. (Grandpa would only curse in these stories if he was quoting someone, and if there were no women present.) Anyway, his borracho friend yells at him.

Deliberately, with impeccable dignity and sangfroid, Pedro parts his arms, mimes giving the beer back. "Ta bueno," he told him. "Hay la tienes. Pero tú ya no me hables más." (Always an ultimatum, unflappable composure in the face of injustice; you have wronged me and the universe will make you pay).

"A year later (see above), se fue pa San Antonio." (His arm sweeps, points grandly to indicate travel. Not here; far, far away).

"Three months later, they brought him back – en un cajón." In a box. Meaning dead. Transgression, rejection, time, retribution. Always retribution, always him shown in the right. Fin. El Jefe's wor(l)d.

And God help you if you asked too many questions. He didn't like me doing that. I'd sometimes do it anyway, because I wanted specifics, nuance, grey tones. I'd rattle the tight confines of his cuentos, his language, and very quickly we'd bump up to the limits of what he remembered (which was often vague, general, fuzzy). When cornered, he'd simply throw up his hands and say, "¿Paqué te digo mentiras? ¡No me acuerdo!" Finally he'd yell at me, huff and puff; he demanded his wor(l)d go unchallenged.[2]

Which makes his one story that deviated from all that, the one that didn't follow any of those patterns, so riveting. No comeuppance for violators, no satisfying vengeance, no balanced scales, no todo o nada — only un mundo de mierda, perseverance, ultimate delivery from evil. This cuento came from a darker, deeper place. I want to set it down as close as possible to the way he told it, that day in 2010 when we all sat around his kitchen table, shortly before Grandma started feeling really sick.

You should know: Pedro was abandoned around six years old by his mother Guadalupe. She ran off with another man. He was raised mostly by his father and an aunt, his tío's wife, Genoveva. This was in south Texas, the Valley in the very old days, when Edinburg was young, much of it still being built. Rural communities, dirt roads, farms. "Allí estabamos en el rancho. Allí había de todo." Pedrito worked, tending goats, cleaning, whatever they told him to do. "Yo mataba pajaritos, conejos." Genoveva would cook them. "Aquí, mijito," le decía.

One thing he often repeated: there by the border they lived with a lot of discrimination. The anglos wouldn't let the Mexican kids on the school bus, or they'd get kicked off. Most never learned to read. Then a man came, "vino un señor, José Alvarado, profesor, me enseñó a mi mucho. ¡Nos crió de burros!" Everyone would laugh when he said that.

Another version: "Yo no agaré educación porque los gringos nos aventaban pa abajo del bos. Y luego entró un profesor, Don José Alvarado. En español sí sé, pero en ingles no. Pues, el ingles lo agaré lírico, hay. Pero no, sta cabrón. Sí, no, sta muy duro. Más antes stava muy duro. Los gringos desgraciados …"

This world, with no justice, where a mother could leave her child and anyone could shit on the poor day after day, shaped his life. But there were sometimes good people, like Don José, who taught him. And Genoveva. She was kind, he said, a good woman. She took care of him, and he loved her.

---

[2] I guess in his own macho way Pedro finally saw me as an equal: when we as a family were discussing his will and who would get what, a couple of years before his death, he turned to me and said, "¿Tú no necesitas nada, verdad? ¿Ya tienes todo, no?" Reir o llorar — I didn't know which.

Then one day, "Genoveva se enfermó, y tuvo loca, y ya."

Longer version: Genoveva's husband, Pedro's tío, was shot. Killed. She lost her mind.

"Porqué lo mataron?"

"Pues, un hombre, borrachos."

"¿En la cantina o qué?"

"Pues, no habían cantinas por allí. No sé donde. Yo estaba muy mediano, pero comoquiera *lo mataron.*" Did I want to hear the story or not? I shut up.

"El señor que mató se fue pa México. Quien sabe donde. Y batallamos mucho nosotros, sufrimos mucho. Pues, Genoveva se enfermó, y tuvo loca, y ya."

With her husband killed, Genoveva gave up. She went crazy. She was yelling and screaming, she stopped eating. She wouldn't say words anymore. She would eat hay or plants or dirt. Smear it on herself. Toda mugrosa. Cagada.

One time they found her sitting on the roof. They had to carefully bring her down. Finally they tied her up in a sort of straightjacket, so she couldn't hurt herself. They kept her with the animals, confined, chained.

Imagine it: Pedrito, terrified, crying, alone again. Tragado por la tierra. Another mother, lost. Only she was still there. But not there. Sufriendo, cada día. No, I can't imagine it.

What could ever make things right?

And then, one day, a man wandered into town from far away, on foot. He had very few belongings. "La curo," he told Pedrito's father and the family. The man needed only three things: a shotgun, an ant hill and a stormy day.

This man (no name was ever given) moved in with them, watched over Genoveva, prayed over her, waiting for the weather to change.

At last dark clouds swirled. The wind picked up. The man went out to an hormiguero. He planted the shotgun, butt-first, next to or on top of it, pointed right at the sky. He moaned, shouted his prayers, right up to God. Ants clung to his boots. Just at the height of the storm, he pulled the trigger, shot at heaven, point-blank. It made a tremendous roar.

And soon after, she got better. Genoveva came back to them. Eventually, she married someone else, moved away lliendo para Chicago. But by then

Pedro was a man, he didn't need her anymore.

And the stranger who saved Genoveva?

"Mi abuelito le dió dos mulas y una yegua por la curación. Era todo lo que tenían, no tenía dinero."

Pedro paused at the end of his story. He looked reflectful. For once, he seemed to have nothing to say.

My grandfather could be a hard man, haughty, prideful, careless of others' feelings. Above all he hated showing weakness. He was the patrón, the paterfamilias, el jefe. He had to always be in charge, with all the answers. He would brook no defiance. My whole life I'd known this about him. El más machote, pues. Which made it all the more astonishing when, for the first and only time in all our years together, I suddenly saw him crying in front of us.

There at his kitchen table, my 90-year-old grandfather's tears streamed down his face, the face of the six-year-old he was, always would be.

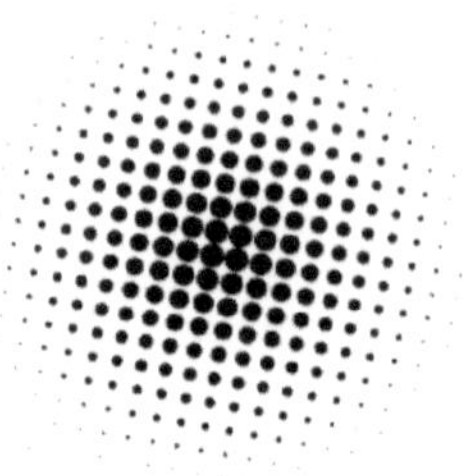

Sandías

1918

"¡I i-i-i-i-i-i-i-i-i-! ¡Que padre, Mami! ¡Que bonitos!"

Pedrito, with all his seven years, screeched and squealed. Just like a javalina. He jostled and jiggled on Mami's lap, the little hairs on his body all on end. His black watery eyes glared up, up, up past Mami's face, past the rocking chair, up past Papi, past the porch, up past the roof, past the zancudos, past the thin glow of the light that came out through the screen door, up and up and up, to the hot black sky. He was watching the fast fast fireflies, dashing down and through and over and all around, like crazy whooshing spitballs. He reached out to touch the fireflies, but they weren't really there. At least, he didn't feel them. Maybe they slipped through his fingers so fast they left no trace. Maybe they burrowed into his hands, buzzed around in there in his veins, sucked some blood como los zancudos, flew out — all in no time at all. ¿Quien sabe? But whatever, the fireflies swarmed all across the sky, leaving streaks of bright color. Red. Orange. Yellow. Blue. Every color Pedrito could name out of his crayon box, and many that he couldn't. But these colors were different. These colors made big buzzing whooshes as they sailed along. Pedrito's eyes filled with reflected streaks and in his ears all those freaky bright whooshes bounced gleefully around. What kind of firefly could do all that?

Meteoritos, the radio called them, said Mami. And because the radio said they were coming, all of Pedrito's friends and his family's friends — all the people Pedrito knew in the world — had gathered there at his porch to greet them.

"Ya vinieron, amigos, ya vinieron," crackled the radio, like through cotton, when you cover your ears with it. "Mira no más. Tan bonito. Gracias a Dios."

Nearby, in the fields, quietly covered with humid night lay la sandía, young and sweet and juicy. It watched and dreamt and grew.

The fireflies crashed and ebbed like waves at the beach. One second there was a great gushing waterfall of millions of drops of colors filling the sky, the next a pallid trickle, like someone turning a big faucet off. Between gushes, Pedrito stole quick glances at his neighbors.

He'd never seen grown-ups act so much like children. They oohed and aahed, they clapped and whistled, they cheered and sang just like jovencitos. Maybe even more alegre, like they found something lost a long long time.

Papi, leaning on the clapboards, puffed madly at his pipe, staring up. Mami rocked the rocking chair and smiled with glazed eyes. The floor creaked. Even Perro, Pedrito's brown mutt, barked and howled at a higher pitch, wagging and working his tail 'til it made a blur in the shadows. Míren, míren, allá, arriba.

There was lots of laughter and making the cross.

Everybody bathed and danced in the falling-starlight.

"Son las lagrimas de Nuestro Señor," said abuelita.

And then it stopped.

For one hanging instant, when the sky emptied, the people held their breath, bit their lips. And then nada. Nada pero nada. The night was dry, bien chupada. God turned off the faucet. No more fireflies.

A few seconds of freefall, and the radio went back to muffled music. The night sounds returned. Someone slapped a zancudo on his shoulder. The crowd dispersed, muttering, "Es todo," giggling, forgetting the feeling of emptiness, glad for a night's entertainment. Tomorrow there was work. In the fields.

Picking ripe, sweet, juicy sandía.

When Mami tucked him in, she ran her fingers over Pedrito's thin, dark body, in his underwear, and made the sign of the cross. Like every night, Pedrito grinned and giggled and whispered his prayers with eyes closed tight, and like every night, Mami smiled and kissed him warmly. But tonight Pedrito was too happy and awake, and Mami looked, even to his young, ignorant eyes, very sad. When she stroked his forehead and wished him good night, and Pedrito said he wanted to play with the fireflies and fly up to the stars, her eyes suddenly watered over. A thin, trembly tear glistened down her cheek. Just like a firefly.

She smiled. Strangely. In a tiny crushed voice she told him to sleep and rushed over to her corner, to Papi's arms — quietly, and for a long time, sobbing.

Huh? Pues, now Pedrito was lost. Even after Mami fell asleep, after she first whispered with Papi for a long time and after she finally turned over. Pedrito still lay there in his bed, on the floor, with Perro breathing on his stomach, trying hard to understand.

Why were people treating him differently? Mami y Papi hardly ever smiled anymore. Only the fireflies had changed that, for a while. Y más y más curioso: they wouldn't let him help with la pisca in the fields, though the other families' children helped like always. Pedrito had to be happy with wiping dirt and dead worms off the sandías. Everybody stared at him with weird eyes, and just smiled as soon as he noticed them. Some mamis wouldn't let their kids play with him anymore. They crossed themselves like they'd seen a demon.

They'd moved to these fields over a moon ago, but Pedrito had no friends. Like they were all staying away — but why?

¿Qué tienen todos?

All he wanted was to play around the sandía fields when the sun had gone down a little, when it wasn't so hot. Chase frogs, with Perro barking and running by his side. But even to this, they said no.

It was like, ever since that old man up north had pricked his skin with a needle and given him a lollipop, and touched him all over with his hands, and shone bright lights on him, and talked for a long time with Mami y Papi in another room, that everything had changed. The more they tried to make it seem like before, the more things felt different. Abuelita talked to God harder, the neighbors came by less, his parents laughed casi nunca. And often, late at night, when they thought he was sleeping, that word would crawl out of their mouths, like a snake or a spider, nesting in their prayers and tears, in their whispers. That ugly, growly word they like it was the devil himself. A word he didn't know. *Tumor.*

Pedrito closed his eyes. Maybe they would all feel better tomorrow. But now, too excited to sleep, his thoughts slipped back to skies llenitas de colored fireflies and buzzing spitballs of light. He smiled and giggled in the dark, talking in a whisper with the fireflies. He invited them to play with his crayons. He offered them sandía to eat. He warned them: no me chupen la sangre.

The idea struck him, suddenly: maybe the radio and everybody was wrong. Maybe the fireflies weren't really gone for good. Maybe they were coming back. Maybe they did want to play with him, now that no one else would. Maybe that's why God sent them. In another second, Pedrito was sure of it. He decided to stay up and wait for the fireflies, as long as it took.

He stared out the open window next to his corner, at the slow drifting clouds. He wiped beads of sweat from his brow and breathed the thick air. Las estrellitas, twinkling. Nearby he could hear the rustle of sandía leaves as they swayed in the warm breeze.

As the night grew más quieta and la luna rolled away, Pedrito's dreams slowly started to fade, grow heavy, sink. His eyes ya no le hacían caso. The drowsiness weighted him down. He slapped himself to stay awake. He strained at the window, seeking out proof he was right.

Nada pero nada.

The yawns came more and more strongly. He was one big yawn. Pedrito frowned, sinking faster and faster. The window and clouds melted into a dark blur. All was quiet, his body relaxed, Pedrito's eyes shut.

And then he heard it. Bzzzzzz.

Much weaker than before, fainter, but it grew louder and louder, echoing in the most distant reaches of Pedrito's mind. Something inside his head knew the sound, shot forward screaming like a mac truck, crashed into wall of his eyes, burst them open.

Through the window, a lonely firefly arched across the sky, buzzing, falling, falling, fell. In the sandía field. The tiniest tremor told Pedrito his eyes weren't lying. The firefly had landed, was lying right now, among the sweet, juicy sandías.

¡Híjole!

He turned to Mami y Papi sleeping in their corner.

"¡M —" he said, then put his hand to his lips, to catch the word. He'd wanted to ask if he could go play with the firefly spitball, but now — no. What would they say? The same thing they'd been saying since they got back from the north. No, they would say. Well, Pedrito could say no también.

He quietly climbed out the window, Perro in his arm. The mutt squealed in confusion. "Shhhh." He put the puppy on the ground. It yawned and wondered where the sleep had gone.

As they walked through the field, Pedrito aimed for the small pillar of glowing dust in the distance. It was farther away than he had thought at the window. The shacks were quiet, everything was still. Only Pedrito, of all the campo, had stayed awake to greet the last firefly. Perro followed him absently, swaying from side to side, tongue out. Except for el oscuro and the receding shacks, there was only the glowing dust, getting closer and closer. Pedrito felt he shouldn't make a sound. He'd surprise the firefly, invite it to play, ask it to take him away to the clouds.

That's what Pedrito thought, in his white T-shirt and underwear, as he approached. And heard a rasping sound, like a truck gasping for gas when people crank it. Perro's ears straightened up. It sounded like breathing.

The air smelled burned. Leaves sizzled. The dust was right before him now. It came from a big, black hole in the ground. There were shattered sandías all around, like broken green eggs with bloody yolks. Their earthy smell mingled with the burned air. Pedrito couldn't see anything but the hole, deep and dark in the cooling dust.

Perro sniffed everything excitedly. The leaves, the ground, the dead sandías. He started growling. Like his nose told him something.

But Pedrito only frowned. Firely? "¿Dónde estás?"

The rasping sound stopped. In the hole was total blackness, Pedrito couldn't see. "¿Estás aquí?" He stepped into the hole, balancing on the rim with his hands. "¿Por qué no hablas?"

He squinted, trying to see, the hole was black, deep black, too black.

Perro barked. Pedrito looked up to him. "Shhh. Cállate. Cállate ya."

Behind the boy, the blackness bagan taking a shape. Like black jello. Pedrito turned, saw it, fell back against the pit wall. The black thing condensed into a liquid column. Then into a small, pointed shape, its beak pointed to him. It kept shifting, flowing like oil. Perro howled and screeched and jumped, falling off the hole's rim, tumbling down next to Pedrito in clouds of dark dust. The black thing reacted with spasms, wincing from them. Then gathered itself for a thrust. It came, shot forth with its beak, all black and featureless but for starlight on its skin.

It fell. Gurgling and rasping, it landed short of the boy and his dog, spasmed, convulsed. It looked like a big black worm now, writhing listlessly. Spreading out slowly, like curdled spilled milk. But black as the gaps between stars.

Pedrito came up close. The thing slowly receded, but only those parts of it he approached. Like ripples in a pond. Perro sniffed and growled, tilted his head.

A flash suddenly struck Pedrito. He blinked, rubbed his eyes. He came closer. Again, a bright burst. Una luz muy bonita. Pedrito looked around, but it wasn't coming from anywhere. For a split second there was light, then he was back in the hole. And it wasn't just light — something moved inside it. The black thing pulled back very slowly, like a snail. Its breathing grew more and more raspy, like an engine that won't start. It was — dying?

The light came again, and with it other things. Sounds, tastes, smells. He recognized the light now; its colors reminded Pedrito of something. In a second he knew.

It was the firefly!

Right in that second, Pedrito was not in the hole anymore. He was nowhere he'd ever been or seen. La luz was all around, de colores: greens, grays, purples, moving all over, colliding. Crackling noises, like the radio, came in and out. Somewhere far, far away Pedrito heard Perro whining, but that wasn't here. That was somewhere beneath this … place, but that didn't sound like the right word.

Pedrito's senses all disagreed. What he saw didn't match with what he felt or smelled, and what he smelled didn't go with the tastes in his mouth. Wind blew his hair. Something warm engulfed him all around, but all he saw was las luzes before him, las luciérnagas, the fireflies. He could still hear the soft sounds of the field at night from afar. It was then that Pedrito saw that the things he was sensing were not from the outside. They came from inside! But inside *what?* The images of luz were in his head; Pedrito knew that his real eyes were seeing something else, but that was blocked by these other pictures. He felt, somehow, like more than one person.

The things that moved in the light came into focus. Mami. Papi. Everyone he knew, doing all the things he'd ever seen them do. Picking, laughing, talking in the night, drinking, fighting, eating sandía con sal y limón. Perro was there too, along with everything Pedrito had ever seen, every place he'd ever been. He saw his life.

But something else moved in there. Walking between his family, standing on abuelita, sharing Mami's body, laughing with his friends, there were the shapes of thin, liquidy, black rubber-band people. They sat next to him when he cut his elbow as a baby; Pedrito felt the pain again, for a brief moment. They cried with him, los elásticos. Pedrito saw them being born alongside Perro, as the puppy came out, wet and tiny, from its mother's back. Pedrito's father shared a cerveza with them, they smiled with him when he said, "Muy abusa'os." They danced with the girls, sliding and bouncing all around them like blacksnakes. They slithered fast in and out of the girls' mouths, came out through the eyes and ears; Pedrito felt their joy. ¡Tan alegres! He smelled strange plants of liquid, glowing purple, saw two red suns in the sky. Sandía grew and flowered everywhere, seeds rained down.

Pedrito giggled. Felt tears streaming down his face. Liquid people, gente elástica, swirled and writhed all over his grandfather's coffin as it lowered to the grave. Music, accordions and birds, so loud his ears buzzed. Loud like thunder, people cried and screamed at the funeral. Weird buildings of water came apart, fireflies flew up to the stars. Pedrito was riding in the truck on his mother's lap along a purple highway. "Michigan, mi'jito," she smiled, her face filling up the world. A rubber-band man was at the wheel.

Moons, like bubbles, whirled by. His father scolded him for breaking a toy. People dying, freezing. Abuelita told him a story about a ghost who gave her an old coin. Stars exploding. The old man pricked Pedrito's arm with a needle, painfully. Balls of air in liquid skin. Music. Colors. Drool on his chin. Burnt air. The world squeezing into a bubble.

Dizzy. Drowning, feverish. ¡Ay Mami! He thought he would burst. Sadness, despair. His life played over and over, la gente elástica clinging, clinging like a ride. A lake of memories. Perro barking. A liquid face, seeping sadly into the earth. A sandía leaf, rolling along the ground in the wind. Hot breath. Night. Smell of cigarettes. Buzzing inside. The feel of his mattress in his corner. Oscuro.

The gray-haired doctor put away his glasses. Packed up his bag. Walked out to his black car with Mami y Papi. Papi helped him crank up the machine that, next to the fields of sandía, looked like it came from another world. The people piscando straightened up from their work to watch. It was late day, la pisca was almost finished. Soon they would all be moving on. Pedrito knew they were talking about him, as they shook hands next to the grumbling carro. Mami stared hard at the doctor, gobbling up his every word. Even from far away he could see her smiling, her eyes watery. The doctor shrugged, bowed respectfully, climbed into the seat. Smoke shot out the machine's back end, it sped down the dirt road, farting fumo.

Pedrito ran among the sandías, kicking up leaves. Perro scampered and barked happily beside him, running circles. The dog was losing its puppyhood, ya. Pedrito collapsed onto a patch of leaves, dirty and sweaty, his neck ringed in grime. How happy it had made him when the doctor said it was okay to play in the fields again. He lay on the ground, looking straight up. The deepest blue filled his eyes.

With a start — ¡híjole! — he saw he was inside the firefly's hole. No one noticed it, because it was all grown over with sandías, thick and leafy and huge, the sweetest Pedrito had ever tasted. He was sure his Papi y Mami would like them too. They were all happy, they thanked Diosito every day.

The firefly nunca volvió. It was gone completely. Pedrito remembered it only in dreams. He stretched and sighed, closed his eyes. The warm breeze and rustle of leaves soon lulled him to sleep. Perro lazed on his stomach, bouncing slowly, up and down.

Pedrito giggled softly with his eyes closed, laughing and running and chasing fireflies in the fields.

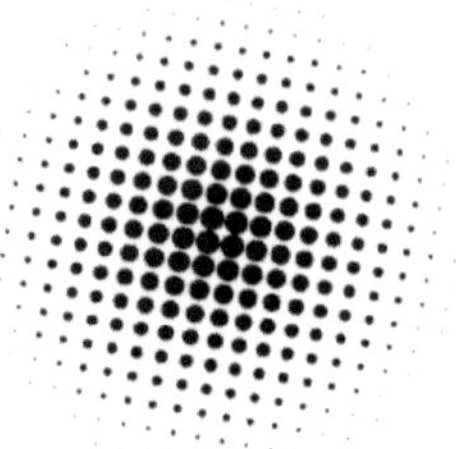

Tamales

2063

El cohete, bent and broken on the Martian sands, orange sands. Strewn eggshells of hull, arced over the horizon. The red sun, wan, sunken, in a pink nest of clouds. The dead ship's jagged shadows. A darkening sky. Slowly darkening. The howls of distant sandstorms, the air, thin air, filled with their hollow drone. The eyes of stars, winking open.

A campfire, fed with rags and cohete offal by the old woman perched on a gray trunk nearby. Her head bent over the flat top of a crate, quivering lightly to the rhythm of her hands. A small mole on her cheek lit up by the lick of the flames, eyes silent and intent. Yellow dough taking shape before her. The movements of her hands, quick, youthful, the dough stretched and flattened into a gooey mass, breathing. A rich corn smell. The husks on another battered trunk, beside her, covered with a strip of cloth slowly gathering dust. The woman's expression, flat and featureless as the desert sprawl, in every direction, to forever. The moan of the wind, a lulling calm. The fire's halo.

"It's done," said the old man, gruffly, descending the crest of a rise. He climbed over cables spilled out of the cohete like seaweed. He picked up the long snake of wires baled together, looked up to the cohete, as if to stuff the tangled strands back into its dark maw. He took a few wobbly steps, when his gaze fell on a small object tangled in the wires — a doll, in a little pink dress. Smiling with rosy cheeks. The old man set the cables down again, angrily, walked on. Each heavy step kicked up puffs of Martian sand, thin puffs. The wind slowly whittled them down to nothing.

"Didn't you hear me? I'm done. It's finished." The old man stood before the fire, removed his cream-colored hat, its inside splotchy with sweat stains. He wiped his brow. "Fucking dust."

The flame's wavering light slid over his face like water as he pounded out sparse orange clouds from his clothes. His tall, lanky body resembled a skeleton: his skin, the texture of rock, stretched tight over the bones, the skull's shape sharp against the purpling sky. The old man scratched his bald head with a sinewy arm. Gazed absently at a mound of disturbed earth several yards away. Replaced his hat. Without his hat he looked and felt unlike himself. Spat. The fire crackled, just audible above the wind.

He turned to his wife. "What are you doing?" He saw. "I told you you're wasting your time, woman. That storm is coming tonight. Can't you hear it? Are you deaf? By morning everything here will be buried twenty feet deep in sand. Us too. Are you listening to me? Are you listening? I said we'll be dead. We'll be dead by the time you finish your goddamn tamales. The storm is coming and we'll be dead, you stupid old ... Didn't you hear? Forget that. I told you anyway I'm not hungry. There's no time for that. Forget it. No hay tiempo."

Amparo stands beside the grave, stiff and erect, as her grandson snaps one picture after another. The December day is cool but half-sunny; she wears her sweater unbuttoned. She is 73. The grass overgreen with juice, freshly mowed. The flowers on the headstone, perfectly arranged. A flawed petal, plucked away, her quick gesture of a bird. As the camera clicks and the grandson shifts positions around her, Amparo adjusts the kerchief over her ears against the wind, lowers her passive, stony face over the immaculate mound.

el cohete sailing smoothly through the dark, its engine's powerful hum perceptible in the black throttle, feeling good in his hands, the distant red orb growing like a spill as he falls, falls towards it, a perfect shot, to the future, the future, to streets he himself will pave with gold ...

— Come here, — he says. The boy starts timidly at the sound. The boy lies in the corner under a sheet, his head on his mother's stomach, his eyes open, with the women, trembling. A skinny thing cringing in the dark.

— I said come here!

the boy hesitates, sees his mother and sisters asleep, then crawls, quivering, across the metal deck, through the hatch, into the tiny cockpit with its dim blinking lights and black oval porthole ... it's so cold in the cohete that the boy's flesh contracts, shrinks, his puny body trying to escape into itself ...

— Take it. Take it, I said. Come on. No es nada. No es nada.

the boy takes the throttle, his hand pulled over onto it by a stronger, surer grasp ... the instrument shakes so violently in his clutch, he has to hold on tight to keep from flying off, he presses down on the round black knob with all his meager weight, the cohete pours its wild, surging power into his body, the boy rattles, crying out feebly as the old man laughs, laughs, his breath fogging up the porthole ...

— That's it! Ha ha! Hold on to it, boy! You're in control now. Keep it steady, I said. You're in control now. Don't let go, or you'll spin us out into the dark. Don't let go, te digo. You want to kill us all before we even get there? Hold on. You're a man now. You're a man. No es nada, I said. No es nada ...

The old man cursed and shouted, kicked at the crushed metal box he'd dragged out of the cohete. He had pried the box open with a strip of the hull's lining he'd crudely bent into an instrument. The makeshift bar bit into his hand. Drops of blood fell onto the sand, Martian sand. Sucked it up greedily. He yelled at the old woman, a string of threats and complaints leveled at her back, her back in silhouette against the fire.

The fire, dying out, fed with scraps of clothing. Pallid smoke, pinkish flame, choked, suffocated in the thin air. No moon on Mars, not even a crescent. But familiar. The desert, familiar. The sand, wind, stars, the same. The flame weak, the stars misty, but the light just enough. Just enough to work by. Dough in her hands, soft and moist, like flesh, corn flesh, rolled around in the bowl, pressed up under her fingernails. The bowl covered with a rag, protected from the sand. Escaped sounds, smells of kneaded dough from inside the bowl, under the rag. The rag from clothing. Women's clothing. A dress. A pile of women's clothing beside her, to feed the fire. A lot of women's clothing now. Girl's clothing.

He stopped up the gash's flow with a pañuelito; a shallow wound, red gleaming fresh against his skin's orange pallor. His hand bandaged, the old man turned to the box. A transparent liquid flowed out of it, joined his blood on the ground, sunk quickly into the parched earth. A penetrating stench rose from the box, along with fizzing noises.

"Fuck, fuck, fuck," he grumbled, reaching into the container with his good hand, moving something around inside. In the end, he found only one bottle intact.

He wiped it off on his shirt. The old man uncapped it and took a long swig, his elbow pointed straight up at the sky. His throat pulsed beneath the skin like some animal. He took the dark bottle from his mouth, ran his tongue along the inside of his cheeks, licked his lips. He did this twice. He then walked over to a point just beneath the cohete's nose. It towered at an angle some thirty feet up from the sand, from where the ship had half-buried itself on impact. He took off his hat. Put it down on a crate. He took out his cigarettes from his shirt pocket, lit one up with an electric lighter. The sun, dull red, snuffed itself out on the wispy horizon. The old man smoked and drank silently, with a vacant expression. He stared before him at a small crater in the earth, slowly filling with a film of wind-borne sand.

The clinic smells of sterile alcohol mixed with urine. Next to Cruz's bed, behind a thin white curtain, lies a man who lost a leg in World War II. The stump, uncovered, is knobbed and obscenely erect. The man watches television with no sound and the empty eyes of a statue. Cruz squirms in his soiled sheets, rumpled like paper. The tongue, an independent thing, glides over his lips, inside his mouth, incessantly. The grandson zooms the camcorder into Cruz's face, its two tiny eyes that seem to have no whites. His hands like claws, like a vulture's or some other carrion bird's; the nurses have put red rubber balls in his palms to keep his fingers from clenching, getting stiff, as if keeping the fingers apart will keep him alive. A tube goes from a slit in his stomach to the suspended placental drip bag that feeds him a white slop. The wisp of hair on his egg-shaped head, the vulture claws, the fetal posture: like some newborn chick, helpless, hairless, awaiting the flutter of its mother's wing, mumbling chirps in a nest of wrinkles. He is 87. His diaper needs changing. Amparo tells her grandson to put his toy down and help her turn him over. He utters vague noises of complaint as he is pushed and pulled and the sheets are replaced, first one side, then the other. Ya, ya, ya, Amparo tells him.

goddamn cocksucking motherfuckers, those bastard coyotes, those fuckers, they told him, they told him the cohete worked, the goddamn cohete would get them there, those fucking hijos de puta, those cocksuckers, those coyotes took their money, a wife and nine kids, but hey, hermano, it's okay, we understand you want to bring them, yeah, bring them over, it's lonely out there, we understand, hermano, fuck you fuck you, everybody's crossing with wives and kids and chickens y todo el chingadero, they're all coming, hermano, those fucking cockroaches called him hermano, yes, fuck you coyotes fuck you and they took his money, yes, and they gave him a goddamn mother-fucking piece of shit cohete that explodes halfway to the other side, those bastards los mato esos coyotes los mato los mato and

el cohete is spinning and steam is blowing out everywhere and alarms are screaming and the girls are screaming and the gravity's gone and bodies are flying and something's burning, it's all burning ...

— Come on, woman! — le grita el viejo, gives her his hand in the mad tumble of hair and arms and legs and luggage and equipment, he holds the boy up against him in the tiny emergency pod designed for one, un cohete designed for six, a cohete stuffed with eleven bodies, those cocksucking coyote fuckers, he holds out his hand and screams at her, the boy screams for her, a thousand different sounds boom and toss them in the dark inside the twisting cohete gone insane ...

— Come on! — he grabs his wife by the hair, by the neck, by the arm, pulls her floating round body into the pod like a bloated balloon, she kicks her feet, struggling, grabs hold of something, her flesh pressed up against them, filling the pod, the warmth of her body, the veins pulsing, engorged, the pod crammed, the boy's puke swimming in bubbles through the air, the hiss of emergency oxygen through the vents, he gropes, blind, for the handle ...

— Get back! No! No room! Get back! — the old man yells, the face of his daughter in the hatch, his daughter, the youngest, barely older than the boy, his daughter and her seven sisters in the cohete's hold, they're choking, burning, slammed against the walls, a hole in the wall, the rush of air bursting out, metal flying, he must close the hatch, la niña screams, cries, begs him, begs him please papi please papi, holds onto the hatch with a tiny brown hand, begging him, but he's caught the handle, he has it he pulls it, he swings the hatch towards the lock, the hatch crushes the little hand, he slams it, the locks engage, the pod is sealed, the three of them are in, outside the sounds are no longer human and the hatch secure and only then does the old woman understand, only then does she react: she screams no, no, no, no, no, her scream louder and louder and louder, no, no, no until her scream fills everything, until the pod becomes her scream

fuck you coyotes fuck you fuck you los mato los mato los mato a todos los mato shut up shut up fuck you coyotes I'll come back and kill you you're dead you're fucking dead fuck you fuckyoucocksuckersyou'redeadyou'realldeadmotherfuckersss

Tamales.
Tamales de carne. Tamales de res. Tamales de puerco. Tamales de frijoles. And the boy's favorite, tamales de azúcar. The nimble work of her hands, their smooth, quick movements, a pinch of raisins poured in each flattened mound of dough, each then folded up and wrapped in a corn husk.
Tamales de pasitas, the boy called them, waiting wide-eyed at the table. A moustache of hot chocolate over his lip. His favorite.

Déjalo morir. Es Dios que lo quiere. Por eso lo hace enfermo. Porque ya lo quiere, que venga ya, que es tiempo ya. ¿Por qué no lo dejas ir? She makes no answer. She stares at him. On her face is no discernible emotion. She stares at him, lying on the reclining bed. Another hospital. Working his tongue. He is 85. She stares at him. She makes no answer.

— No. No. No se arrimen.
el viejo mumbles in his sleep, turns over angrily. Scowling, pulling the metallic sheets closer to his body ...
— No, he mutters, no, I said, no. Get back. No. Go away. Go away.
the boy, a medi-patch on his forehead, holding on to his mother for warmth, watches his father, listens to the indistinct sentences, his eyes two watery points reflecting the pallid light of stars over this dark world, so quiet, everything so quiet, nothing makes a sound, nothing, nothing loud filling up his ears, no explosion, no tearing of metal, no whoosh of air, no thunderous crash, no screams, nothing, nothing makes a sound, not his mother shivering in her sleep, not his sisters lying in their mound of

Martian sand, not the cohete snapped in two like a bone, not the smashed radio drained of static, its batteries dead, not his muscles aching from a day of digging, hauling, searching, not even his own heart, beating, beating so quiet, everything so quiet, so still, except the old man, el viejo mumbling, barking at the shadows inside him, tossing beneath the metallic blanket he refuses to share, the old man's squeaky voice of a bat, bouncing weakly on el cohete's broken walls that let in starlight, the old man warm under his silver sheet but still he's mumbling like a child, as the boy watches, silently, the old man mumbling, mumbling

— Go away. No. No.

With a sullen look, he undid the doll from its tangled prison of cables. In the campfire light its red hair made ragged shadows along its face, which smiled up at him. He sucked on his foul-smelling cigarette, filling his lungs with its filth. Stared at the doll. It escaped the crash without injury, without even a scorch mark or stain of blood. There had been no need to sift through the wreckage for it, no need to pull its burned meat in strips from the cohete's hold. No need to salvage its dress for fire fuel, to take it, trying not to gag, piece by piece, limb by limb, in crisp pulpy heaps to the pit, no need to toss it in, a mass of rags and bone and curdled organs like jellyfish, and cover it up with sand. The doll had simply lain there in its nest of wires, waiting for him to find it, smiling and happy.

The old man took the doll to the fire, stood impassively, gazed at the flames. Threw it in. In a minute it had melted into brown slag and plastic smoke, noiselessly. Again he noticed the stormhowl, unending, rising. Irritated him. The wind was getting stronger, louder. The sand leaping up, catching the wind, slowly choking the fire. His body tensed, like a rusty spring. The storm. Gritted his teeth. Eyes narrowed to black slits at the storm he couldn't see, only feel, hear, taste its sand on his lips. The rage coursed through his veins, like the booze, the cigarette's filth, warm, electric. Suddenly he coughed, spit out the particles of sand, the rage flaring. He turned to his wife, still sitting uselessly at her makeshift kitchen, huddled near the fire.

The tamales simmering in the pot, suspended over the fire, rocked lightly by the wind. Tucked in their corn husk beds, the tamales submerged in the hot water, in layers, added slowly, first one layer, then another on top, then another, then another. Not long. Not too long. The boy would wait, swinging his legs in his seat. Not long. Long enough for the dough to harden, congeal, for the pasas and sugar to heat up. For when the dough no longer sticks to the husk. The water at a simmer, only a simmer. Not too much flame. Just enough. Just a little. When the dough no longer sticks, they're ready. Almost ready, mi hijito. The tamales, almost ready.

"I told you to stop that," growled the old man. Flung his cigarette into the fire. Kicked up more dust into the wind. Lumbered towards her.

He wanders the town, a stooping old man in a cream-colored hat like any other. Booze, bad cigarettes on his breath. The bars, rich people's houses where he mows yards for beer money, 6 a.m. Sunday mass, his daughters' homes. He comes every week, sits in the kitchen, mumbling for hours in a squeaky, irritating voice, about things his grandchildren casually ignore. They nod, fidget, waiting for their mother to quietly gesture, freeing them from this prattling viejito to the release of the television. Even their mother fidgets, finally tells him she has an errand to run, slips money in his hand at the door, payment for an afternoon's boredom. He leaves, his bent-over lope. Sometimes he walks along the very middle of the road. He starts asking his grandchildren for money, in a mumble they can barely make out now. Only Amparo understands. Amparo just knows he has another woman, though he is well past 70. "Por ay tiene una vieja," she tells her grandson. "Don't give him money. No le des. He'll just spend it on his vieja cantiñera." "Mentiras," he mutters, scowling weakly in his armchair. Their house grows quiet. The daughters are married, scattered. He keeps the lawn tidy. Grandchildren and great grandchildren. The son, the youngest, lives with them, slowly drinking himself to death, bearing the brunt of Cruz's worst deprecations, half-uttered now through toothless gums. Every year the son sinks deeper and deeper into himself, away from his father, away from everything, down the numbing spiral. More and more, Cruz has trouble remembering things, except for a past he cannot articulate, in which his descendants take no interest.

— Son of a bitch! — the old man yells as he slips. He falls from the cohete's metal rib that snaps beneath his weight. He falls on his elbows, his face plunging into the orange sand, as the boy, watching at a distance, near his mother, sees his father fall from atop the cohete and suddenly, sin querer, the boy laughs ...

the old man curses, shakes off the powdery dust, thinking, thinking he needs to climb up there, he needs to see, the radio, before it died, the radio warned of the storm, stuck in the Martian desert on a goddamn coyote's cohete chingado and the satlink useless and the radio before it died warned of the sandstorm and the land is too flat, and the old man is thinking, thinking that he has to get up there to see, to el cohete's tip, to see where the storm is, from up there you can see for miles, he's thinking, thinking he has to get up there but he can't, the metal's too thin, he's thinking, sweating, wiping his brow in the yellow heat, thinking how to get up there, thinking about the cohete's nose, and then the boy's laugh rings in his ears as the wind picks up and the reddish sun stands right at the tip of the cohete ...

— Ven pa cá, — the old man commands. — Ven pa cá, I said.

"I told you I don't want any!" he yelled at her. "Stupid puta! What good are your tamales now? We're dead, I said! We're dead! We're already dead!"

The night wind shrieked louder all around him as he pulled her by the wrist away from her trunk, as he pushed her down to the earth, as he proceeded to kick and tear and break apart her dishes, turn over the crate, spill the dough and husks and rags onto the ground. Watching, her face never changed expression.

"We're dead, mujer. We're all dead! Fuck your tamales de mierda! What good are they now? What good are they now?"

He grabbed the metal pot and screeched, his hands burnt. The pain stopped his thinking, the rage swelled, he lashed out, reasonless, kicked at the large metal pot with his boot, as the wind gusted, as la vieja lay where she'd been thrown in the dust, as the howl filled his ears.

The pot spilled onto the fire as the old man lost his balance, the water met the flames with a loud hiss, throwing up clumps of half-burned fuel, debris and clothing that the wind flung upwards — into his face. The fire crackled, blazed as it devoured the husks, the dough, discharging a sickly-sweet smell of corn, sugar, pasas giving up their juice, smoldering.

The old man screamed, his hands pressed to his face, seeming to dance with the flames all about his legs. He screamed as he fell away from the fire, his hat flying, rolling, snatched away by the ravenous wind, the old man kicking and twisting, his scream mingling with the wind, swinging one lanky arm wildly all about him, feeling his fist strike soft flesh, struggling like an animal as he felt his burning trousers doused with sand, felt the arms of his wife trying to pull his hands away. He pushed himself from her, still swinging his fist, and turned, buried his forehead in the cool sandy earth, screaming, screaming, feeling his mouth fill up with dust as the spitting sparks in his eyes died away to blackness.

They cross the river, the whole family, the shallow part at midnight, because Cruz is tired of going back and forth. The coyotes are kind, they offer their own secluded house near the river on the other side, to hide them, give them a place to sleep. The coyotes are kind, an old man and his son, but they are still coyotes and they demand a stiff price. Strong and healthy at 35, Cruz works in a steel factory in Pennsylvania, but quits when the smoke starts to poison his lungs, as it did his brother's. He does not give up his tarry, unfiltered cigarettes, though. They pick vegetables, migrate with the seasons: Louisiana, Ohio, Michigan, California, and back to Texas. The whole family works, living in company shacks. They fight horribly, but never lay a hand on the children. Cruz only yells and terrifies them into submission, taking out his belt for those who insist on disobedience, the ones who sneak out to meet boys in the town behind his back. Once a week he takes them for a burger and a movie. That should be enough for them. The family saves up to buy a house; finally, they settle. En fin Amparo gives him eight children, the last the only son.

the boy doesn't want to, he tells his father, he doesn't want to, he's saying, I can't do it, please don't make me do it, he hangs his bandaged head before the old man in front of the cohete, the sun bearing down on his scrawny frame, but the old man won't stop pushing him, telling him to climb up there, he's the only one, he has to climb up there and tell him where the storm is, it's nothing, he says, it's nothing, el cohete's ribs will hold you, so get up there, it's nothing, and the boy tries to look up at his father but the sun burns his eyes, its flash filling up his vision and he sees only a hard silhouette with a hat looming over him, the blinding sun over its shoulder, he can't see, but he says please in his tiny voice and the old man pushes him, saying no es nada, no es nada, you'll go up and come down, what's the matter, you act like a girl, you act like your dead sisters, get up there, it's nothing, I said, get up there and show me where the storm is this land is too flat ...

the boy, hesitating, slowly climbs up the rib of the cohete, unsteady, the hot sun making little circles in his vision, looking with wide eyes back at his mother, round and sad by a heap of clothes, as the old man tells him see, it's nothing, I told you, it's nothing, go higher, I said, it's nothing ...

The wind's howl, deafening now. Swirls of dust, spinning all around, the fire long dead. The stars, snuffed out. Black, strangulating sand. The old man, his eyes tenderly bandaged, and the old woman, supporting him, the two before a tiny heap of earth, disintegrating in the gale. Just visible in the shifting, baying murk, a white cross made of cohete pipes.

On their wedding night the sheet is stained with a faint red splotch. Afterwards he commands her to take the linen outside and wash it, in the darkness. With every motion of her hands on the cloth she feels the painful wet rip inside her, moving. She washes the spot clean away and returns to him.

the boy balances on the very nose of the cohete, his father and mother now small enough to hold in his hands, Mars grown massive and flat in all directions, he a tick on the bump of a huge orange ball, the sun feeling good on his face now, the wind, the thin air, he giggles, giddy, looks about for the storm like his father tells him, look around, he says, tell me where the storm is, he stretches, strains out to see more of the horizon, looking for the storm, his father was right, no era nada, easy, he's so light, he cranes his neck in all directions, no es nada, the wind pleasantly in his hair, he hears

he hears his mother yelling something, his father, calling out to him, he hears the creak, feels the swaying of the cohete, something somewhere snapping

and the boy slips, he falls, falling, falling more slowly in the Martian gravity, reaching out frantically, convulsing, spinning, tumbling like an injured bird, down, down, the earth rushing up in a final flash of the sun

before the muffled, sickening snap ...

la vieja hardly moves, takes a few steps, stops, stares at the cloud of orange dust by el cohete, her husband shuffling towards it, throwing up more dust behind him, staring vacantly she feels something go, and without a word, a sound, without anything at all, she collapses on her knees in the sand.

Cruz sees her at a village dance, a peasant girl. He is nearly 30, the son of a bandleader. A hard man who breaks horses. An Appaloosa is his favorite. She is not yet 15, a thin girl with black hair like any other, with a name that pleases him. He will take her. Maybe someday he can bring her with him, al otro lado. Her name is Amparo. Un nieto, nacido allá, would confuse her name with "lámpara" — lamp — and think of her as light. Only later would he know amparo does not mean light. Amparo means "shelter." Amparo.

— It was nothing, I told him, just go up and come down, I said, that's all, that's all, just go up and come down, — says the old man, talking as he's done for the last hour, mumbling, shouting, saying the same things again and again, saying it's not my fault, you hear, it's not my fault as he pats down the mound with his shovel and starts to fashion his crude cross and bends his head, listening for the wind, but talking, talking, grumbling all the time ...

the old woman sits by the grave, staring at the fresh, dry earth, unmoving, thinking, thinking of something, thinking of getting up, of finding her pots and bowls, and the other things she'll need ...

she's thinking, thinking of tamales ... tamales de azúcar, the boy's favorite ... tamales de azúcar ...

The sandstorm, a blanket of bees, angry, stinging, buzzing, loud. Everything, everything penetrated by the sound, bones, shaking, pierced. Wind. El cohete, coming apart like straw. Metal, memory, flesh, shredding, dissipating, absorbed. Hot Martian sand, lungfuls, burning. Parched throats in the lost hollow of a broken, crumbling cohete. Tears.

El viejo in her arms, head on her bosom: statues, sand-swallowed, cooling, softening, whittling, blanched. El viejo, tight in her embrace, la vieja, cuidándolo. In her body's fragile shelter.

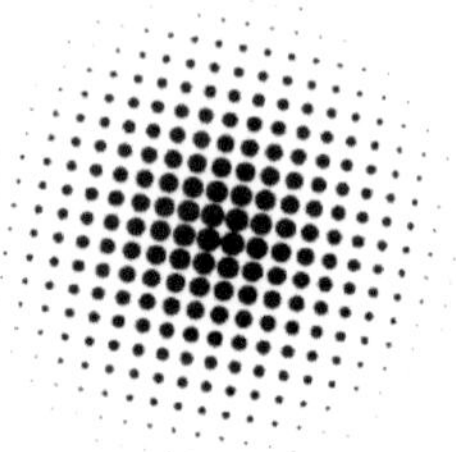

La Tormenta

1968

"Hurricane Delilah" slammed into the Valley on January 17, 1968, at about 11:15 p.m. Although not a real hurricane (hurricane season having already been over several months), this freak winter storm brought with it 40-mile-per-hour winds, floods, power shortages, and general misery. The fierce pounding lasted only a few hours, but the storm's surprising strength caught a lot of people unprepared. There were news reports of kids going to the hospital for shock, and a couple of elderly folks suffered heart attacks.

But the storm went down in the record books and local lore for another reason: Delilah brought to the Valley, for the first time anybody could remember, tennis ball-sized hail. We're talking about an area that experiences a freeze maybe only once every few decades. Most of the locals, except for the migrant farm workers, had never seen snow in their lives. People freaked out when they saw white gobs of ice plummeting out of the black, angry clouds, smashing into windows, sidewalks, roofs. The sky was falling.

According to Valley legend, a piece of the sky smacked everybody's favorite chimp at Gladys Patten Zoo right in the eye, causing the frightened animal to slip from its perch on a jungle gym and snap its neck when it hit the ground. The chimp's name was Delilah, and that's how the storm got its name. People didn't forget it anytime soon. Delilah was so violent in parts of Villa county that some of the devout swore it was Christ's second coming, a claim they usually reserved for especially strong hurricanes.

In the middle of all that chaos, Joe decided to enter the world.

His paternal grandmother, Concepción Alonzo, told me the story. Fortunately, by the time we spoke I'd honed my Spanglish to a level sufficient to understand her.

"Sí, mi hijo. I remember it. How could I forget? Not only did the family gain a son that night — it almost lost a grandmother. That was so long ago, but yes, I remember. I couldn't sleep that night. I don't know why. Pero este hombre, my husband, Joe's grandfather — he can sleep through anything, so he didn't hear the thunder or anything. One minute it was dry and still, just thunder far away, then the wind starts to pick up, and it got colder, and the rain begins, like buckets. I turned on the radio and heard it say that it was a storm, one that they hadn't expected. I remember I crossed myself when I went out to see, still in my nightgown in the back yard porch, and said, 'Ai, Diosito mio,' when I saw the clouds swirling, turning, like they were alive. The clouds looked blacker than the night itself. There were no stars, no moon, anywhere.

"I brought my cat inside and made sure our two dogs were safely under the porch roof. I've forgotten their names, they all died long ago. But I remember sitting in a rocking chair with the cat purring in my lap, watching the storm get worse, and the rain get harder, in the dark. The cold air felt good on my forehead, but I quickly closed the window because I didn't want to catch cold. The rain was very loud, like in a hurricane. The wind noise reminded me of an engine running, and I thought about something my grandmother had once told me when I was a little girl, crying and scared during a storm. She said that God spoke in the wind, that the wind was his voice, but only the brave and the dead could hear it. I sat there rocking the chair for, I don't know, maybe two hours.

"Then the phone rings. It was my son, Mex, calling from his apartment. Raquel, Joe's mother, had started having contractions about 40 minutes before. Mex said they'd already been to the hospital, and the doctor said she was already dilated five centimeters. 'Pues, qué haces en casa?' I scolded him. 'Why are you at home?' He said that Raquel wanted to take care of some things before going back, that she said she didn't feel that bad. It was her third child, so she could tell she had time. I was still angry at him for letting her leave the hospital, especially in this storm. That woman has always been so stubborn. Terca, I always called her.

"Mex said they wanted to drop off the kids here on their way back to the hospital and I said 'tá bueno, but hurry up. Then I woke up este hombre. The rain was falling even harder now.

"I didn't see Raquel when they stopped by, because she stayed in the car and waited while Mex brought Yolanda and Pete over through the lluvia, the rain. I saw Pete drop a coloring book or something onto the wet pavement, it just blew out of his hands, and he tried to pick it up. 'Leave it!' Mex told him, and dragged him by the arm. In seconds the booklet was soaked, battered down by the rain.

The children were sleepy but excited. ''Ello, Gran'má,' Yoli said. 'I'm gonna have another baby brother.' They crowded around me, holding on to my nightgown. They were only about eight and seven then. Mex smiled at me in the doorway — I remember seeing his face, his moustache, lit up by the lighting — y le dije, 'Con cuidado. Está muy peligroso en las calles,' and he said, 'Sí, 'Amá.'

"A few hours passed. Mex called every half hour. They had made it to the hospital alright through those terrible streets slick with rain. Raquel was having stronger and stronger contractions. Mex said the hospital had lost power for about a minute, but everything was fine. Yoli and Pete were playing a card game, with the cat on Yoli's lap. They had slept a little, but now the loud rattle of the rain was keeping them awake. Even este hombre kept complaining he couldn't sleep.

"And then, suddenly, there was a horrible slap of thunder, terribly loud, it felt like it had hit inside the room. And the power went out. We all screamed together in the dark. I saw the cat running out of the living room, his tail in the air, lit up by lightning. One of the windows had a large crack in it. I went up to it to look outside. Dios mio. One of our trees had been hit. A main branch had been torn off by the lightning. It was barely hanging on, shreds of it, clinging to the tree, blowing in the wind. The trunk was scarred black. I was about to tell este hombre about the tree when we heard these loud bumps on the roof, RAT-TAT-TAT-TAT.

"That's when I noticed este hombre coming in from the kitchen with a flashlight in his hand. 'Quítate de allí, Concha! Quítate! Get away!' he kept saying. I heard the wind change its tone, and then there was the sound of glass shattering and the storm flew into the room. Yoli screamed. Pieces of the window were all over my back, for some reason they reminded me of ants. It was cold. We quickly herded the children out of the living room.

"The glass hadn't hurt me, gracias a Dios. But my nightgown was soaked along the back. The children laughed at Grandma all wet, it helped to calm them until the light came back. Sometimes I think about what might have happened if I hadn't turned away from the window at that moment, to call out to Pedro. What that glass might have done to me if I had been looking right at it. Pero Diosito nos cuida, nos cuida todo el tiempo. Don't ever forget that.

"After I changed and este hombre put some board up over the window, things calmed down. Pedro, my husband, said it was granizo that had crashed through the window, and I was so stupid I didn't even know what that was. Granizo? 'Piedras, mujer, piedras de hielo,' he said to me, angry. I crossed myself and thanked Diosito again.

"I sat in the kitchen, Pedrito sleeping on my lap. Yoli lay in an armchair under a blanket. Pedro was snoring in the bedroom. El granizo had stopped long ago, it didn't last very long at all, but the wind kept howling. I got the phone call sometime after 2:30. Joseito was born. Everything was fine. I told Mex what had happened and said we were all fine and we'd go see them in the morning. Still holding Pedro, I went over to Yoli and whispered to her, 'Ya tienes un nuevo hermanito.' She smiled, sleepily, then made a slight frown.

"'Qué te pasa?' I asked. 'The wind won't let me sleep,' she said. 'It's so loud. It scares me.' And like a wheel turning somewhere, like something sliding into place just right, I knew exactly what to say. I told her God spoke in the wind, it was God's voice, and only the brave and the dead could hear it. She smiled, her eyes closed, and soon drifted off to sleep."

There were, of course, other points of view that night — Joe's mother Raquel's most obviously comes to mind — but Concha's story seemed the most appropriate to me, somehow. It was certainly the most dramatic.

Raquel told me that the birth was easy; four pushes and Joe was out. It was all the commotion and worry about the storm that made things seem worse than they were. "But, really, it was no trouble," she said. "He was a beautiful baby boy, five pounds, three ounces. Even the doctor liked him." Maximino, Joe's dad, remembered talking to another expectant father in the waiting room that night to pass the time. That man's baby actually died later that day, after being born. He didn't remember why.

And so, that's how Joe entered the world, on the waves of a violent "hurricane" that nearly killed his grandmother and did kill the Valley's favorite chimp. I guess Joe's and Delilah the chimp's souls passed each other in the ether that night.

Incidentally, 1968 was a year of the Monkey in the Chinese zodiac.

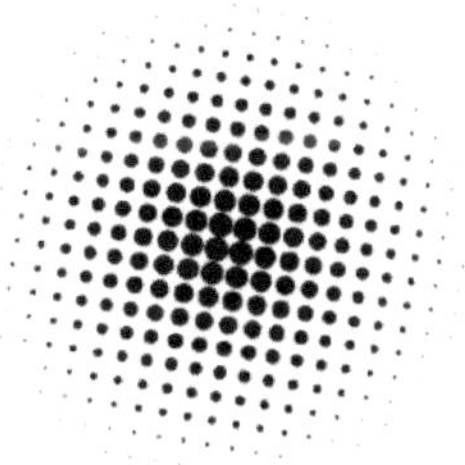

Solito

1972

I can recall three incidents from my childhood which I feel contributed to what I would term my sense of self-reliance, my disinclination to get too dependent on anybody for anything.

The first is one of my earliest memories (though come to think of it, these are all early memories), which took place, I suppose, when I was five or six (a simple inquiry would fix the date). My mother was in the hospital (much later I learned, in order to undergo a hysterectomy) and I hadn't seen her in a while (it may have been for only a couple of days). I was told that she would be coming home the next day, and so I had my grandmother or someone buy me a glass ash tray in the hospital gift shop, as a sort of homecoming present. I remember the next day as bright and shining and hot outside, and I stood in the entryway to our house, holding the gift behind my back, ready to surprise and delight my mother when she came in. She would see me, hug and kiss me, and be warmly touched by my thoughtful present. I stood there, swinging on my heels as I saw through the window the car driving up, and saw her get out. She was wearing a blue robe and seemed to be walking a little unsteadily.

She came in. I beamed. She walked past, started barking orders, and gave me only the slightest pat on the head. She said the house was a mess and now that she was back she was going to get everything in order. She didn't even stop to hug me and did not give me a chance to present my offering. I remember a feeling of hollowness, not exactly disappointment, although I guess that's the only word for it. A hollow, empty place where my realized childish fantasy should have been. Later that night, I brought the ash tray to my Mom while she was lying down, smoking in her bedroom, and she actually was pleasantly touched by the gift, and did kiss me and hold me. But by then (and maybe this is a retrospective pronouncement) her affections didn't matter as much. I had already been let down, and it had taught me a lesson: that people, often through no overt fault of their own, will not always understand or appreciate it when you try to reach out to them. They had their own concerns, their own agendas, which could be and often were quite unrelated to mine, and indeed, this was as it should be. It was just one of those things.

The second is similar in some ways but more traumatic, because it involved tears. I was with my family in Reynosa, and somehow me and my Dad split off from the others (it could be we had gone to get our hair cut, which we did in Mexico back then). We were walking along a crowded street, in the mercado area near the town square. I was, I don't remember, very young, again, maybe five or six. I walked behind my father and kept stepping on his heels. The sidewalk was so packed with people that we couldn't really walk side by side, so he told me to walk in front of him. I was a little leery of this, since it would mean that I couldn't see him and know he was there. But I did as he said. We walked on to wherever we were going, and from time to time I looked back to make sure my father was still with me in this crowd of scary strangers.

Finally, one time I looked back and he was gone. I panicked and looked everywhere for him, but the crowd was so dense, there were so many shuffling, gigantic figures hurtling by, that I felt almost claustrophobic and could see little around me besides bodies. I walked along the street, timidly, looking for my father in a mass of faces. I called him and turned this way and that, not finding him, lost, alone. I started to cry. I don't know how much later (it was probably only a few minutes), I saw my father emerge from the crowd in the distance, on the opposite side of the street. He was walking towards me, smiling, waving, looking completely at ease and unworried, as if he somehow knew that I would be alright without him. His utter calm in the face of what to me had been a catastrophe was what startled me perhaps more than anything else. To my recollection, he made no mention of noticing my tear-stained face. I didn't hate my father (just as I hadn't hated my mother for initially ignoring my gift), but I once again felt that, ultimately, I was alone; that I had no one to really count on but myself. This was a sobering but not, as I recall, distressing fact. At least, it didn't distress me for too long. My Dad, while unperturbed at my absence (he said he had stepped into some store somewhere), was happy to see me; we went along merrily to join the rest of the family and had a fine time the remainder of the afternoon.

The incident, in retrospect, had proved conspicuous only for its normalcy.

Finally, the episode that I feel probably cemented this "alone in a void" attitude, because it was exactly like the others, only moreso; more universal, so to speak. I was to spend the day in the care of my grandparents. I must have been no older than in the other episodes, and perhaps much younger. I'm not even sure that I could articulate words very clearly at the time, so I might have been very young indeed. My father dropped me off at my grandparents' house in the truck, it was morning. I had with me a box of toys, action figures and stuff, to play with. There might have been some kind of misunderstanding, or maybe my father simply didn't wait in the truck to be sure, but it turned out my grandparents weren't home. I knocked and knocked at their door, but no answer came. My father had driven off; I might have given him the "okay" sign without thinking, or as I said he might simply have not waited for it. I don't remember. I was alone — in fact, I don't think I've ever felt more alone in all my life as I did during that time. I sat down in the front porch with the box of toys in my lap, getting more and more worried, more and more desperate, and actually trembling. I had never been without an adult or my sister to take care of me, and now there was no one there. I felt that sensation of hollowness again, that oppressive feeling of something very necessary and vital being completely and utterly missing. Where could they be? How could they have done this? What on earth could I possibly do? Everything suddenly seemed terrifyingly large and I appallingly small. The plants and fronds in the front porch loomed over me, like lions, I remember. I started shaking, shaking with tears. I turned to my helpless toys; they looked inert and dead and powerless to help me. They were now just simplistic childish figures molded from plastic, rattling in a box to the motion of my sobs. Finally, in desperation, I decided that I had to get back home somehow. I had to be with others to care for me, I had to escape this horrifying solitude. Slowly, unsteadily, I got up and walked out onto the front driveway, through the chain link fence gate, and stared at the wide street, having only the vaguest idea which way home lay. I had never, through countless car rides, paid attention to which streets we were on, which direction we drove in; in my infantility I'd been all but oblivious to such incidental trivia. Now I cried and cried in my ignorance, and started on the path I thought and hoped would lead back home. I walked along Sprague street, in roughly the right direction, but with every step I got more scared and cried harder, the toys bouncing and rattling in their box as I clung to it, pathetically pressed it against my chest. Cars drove past, there might even have been a stray bicyclist, but no one stopped to help, and I didn't ask them to. Life around me went on unbothered, unconcerned (as it should be) with my tragedies. Despite the terrible experience of walking down that gigantic street that seemed to stretch crushingly forever into the distance, despite my hot tears and pitiful moans, I knew somehow, now that I reflect on it, that this was all, in an ultimate, undeniable sense, the most perfectly natural thing — and maybe that was why I cringed and cowered and flailed so much, because all this was inevitable, unchangeable, the cruel (?) but necessary order of things. Perhaps there's just no easy way to learn this; the lesson, by its very existential nature, is traumatic: I was of the world, but not central to it, part of this community, but in the most perversely natural sense, I, like everyone else, was absolutely and forever on my own. This was good because this was truth.

So, shaking in my sneakers, driven by terror to a kind of resigned depression, I gave up my quest for home after some 50 yards and shrunk back to my grandparents' porch, where the world, after all, did not end and my sobs soon died down to nothing. Calm. My grandparents came before long, of course. I had, in all likelihood, been left alone no more than half an hour; they had been having lunch at a nearby center for elderly people that served cafeteria-type food. I told them, bravely, as composedly as I could, that my father had dropped me off and that I'd been waiting for them in the porch "un ratito." My grandmother wiped my face, wonderingly, saying, "Tienes la cara choreada," and she asked me if I'd been crying. I lied, but it was hardly a secret.

The rest of the day was spent normally, with my smiling, revived toys, and under the attentive gaze of grown-ups. But inside me the seeds of doubt, of solitude, of self-reliance, had already sprouted.

By the time I was seven or eight, I had grown quite used to being on my own; as a latch-key child with his television and comics (and occasionally a friend), I could not have had a happier childhood. This is not to say I did not depend on my parents for everything, of course, from my clothes to my dinner to my Hulk, but emotionally I (and they) was already growing quite distant, independent. My mother raised us with a very loose, free hand, and my father was even more remote, with me, at least. This arrangement crystallized into the Normal Order of Things in my family, and it was only in extreme circumstances, or when our way of life bumped into another, that I even noticed it. A good example is when l was walking home once, swinging some newly — purchased comics in a paper bag (I remember one of them was *Ms. Marvel* number 4, which dates this incident to sometime in 1977). Striding obliviously along a rarely-taken but not unfamiliar street, I was atttacked by a large dog. The damn thing started barking and bolted across its yard toward me, and though at first I couldn't quite believe what was happening, a couple of seconds later I took off, literally running out of my shoes, moving faster than I'd ever moved in my life. The dog bit me on the shin anyway. I got home, head and heart still pounding (but still holding on to Ms. Marvel) and showed the injury to my mother, who lay in bed. She gave it a cursory glance, and pronounced it not serious. A little disinfectant and a band aid later, I was well enough to go visit my grandmother. For some reason, my mother had not made any big deal out of my losing the shoes. But my grandmother, well, she almost had a heart attack when I told her what had happened. Prone to over-reacting to things to this day (and always ready to challenge her daughter-in-law's authority over her grandchildren), she demanded we go to the hospital, get me checked out for rabies (they gave me a shot) then proceed down to the dog's house, complain to the owners, and retrieve the shoes.

There they were, strewn along the street at various angles, like slain brown soldiers on a battlefield. My grandmother angrily denounced the family who lived there, which was an embarrassing, tiresome affair for me, all the more so since they just happened to be in the minority of Valley residents who were white and didn't speak Spanish, so I had to translate Granmá's tirade and their replies back and forth. The family of gringos were nonplussed, not sure what the big deal was now that I'd gotten the shoes back and they saw the bite on in my leg was not severe. The guilty dog, in fact, was now acting very friendly, waving its tail and barking with glee. All in all, it was a pretty surreal, uncomfortable and absurd afternoon.

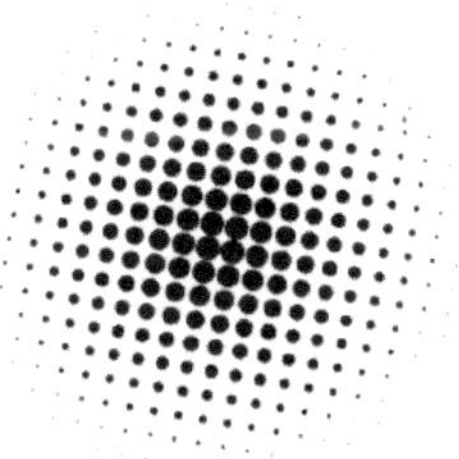

The Bike

1978

The only time my father ever got angry with me, and came close to hitting me, was when I lost my bike. He had told me not to leave it in the front porch, where it could get stolen, and park it instead in the backyard, behind the red fence. I disobeyed him, and one morning the bike was gone. I think I discovered this before him, but for some reason didn't believe it would amount to anything; our family was pretty lax about such things, and in my seven or eight years of life my father had never punished me for anything before.

Besides, the bike was just a cheap, ugly, battered banana seater I'd ridden way beyond its useable lifespan, and that'd had its dorky upright flagpole thingie broken by some neighborhoodlums (a story in itself).

Anyway, I was in my sister's room (I spent a lot of time with my sister in those days, even slept in the same bed with her, something I think my father somehow thought was improper for a grown boy. So when he saw me there on the floor with her, playing some childish game or listening to 78's, it somehow fueled the ensuing scene further, I think). I remember sitting on the floor (?). My father stormed into the room, in a rage. I'd never seem him like that. I don't remmeber whether he said much. He was angry about the stolen bike, of course. He must have reproached me for not listening to him.

He picked me up violently by the back of my shirt and pulled me out of Yolanda's room. I thought he was going to spank me, which he would often do to my delinquent brother but had never done to me. I rememebr feeling pretty fatalistic about it, like Henry in *Goodfellas* ("The way I saw it, everybody gets a beating sometime"). But he didn't hit me. He dragged me to my room (and my brother's) and threw me on the floor and told me I couldn't leave, I was grounded (don't think he used that word). He slammed (?) the door and stormed out. Actually he might have said something like, "¡Chingao! ¡Te dije!".[3] He really was mad. It was odd and I suppose scary, but like I said I was very accepting of the whole thing. Obviously I'd gotten off with a light sentence. I was, of course, sorry to see the bike go, even if it was a piece of shit (though at that time I wouldn't have expresed myself like that). I rrremember the frame was an ugly purple color and the plastic seat had a glittery sort of design to it. I loved that bike, I realize now. But it was gone, I was grounded (or more literally, floored, and even more literally, *rugged* onto the wooly orange circle in the middle of my room) and that was that.

The story has a happy first epilogue. Some weeks (?) later I walked over to grandma Concha's house, just two blocks from ours, and there I saw Dad in a lawn chair on the driveway. It was late afternoon or maybe evening. He had just gotten back from a business trip (hauling vegetables? buying used cars?) and this was the first time I'd seen him in perhaps a few days (these trips never lasted too long, as I recall). The scene was rather enchanting and also rather sad, reconstructed from this low angle of my memory, walking slowly along the green, juicy grass of my grandmother's front lawn in the shade of her house's roof, with my father sitting there, smiling beatifically. Why was he smiling so? He seemed as disproportionately happy now as he'd been enraged then. "Mi'jo," he said to me as I climbed up the steep incline of the driveway towards him, "te trayí algo."[4]

Or no, I think it was the even more tender "Te trayí *a*lgo, mi'jo," with a sweet, enticing lilt on the fourth syllable. He hugged me, still sitting in the lawn chair. I don't know if anyone else was there. Probably grandpa. Now that I think of it, this was perhaps one of the most loving moments I ever shared with my father as a child. Why such nice treatment, such emotion? Did he kiss me?

---

[3] "Fuck! I told you!"

[4] "Son, I brought you something." Actually, he probably didn't say "trayí," but "traje," which is more standard Spanish, but for some reason that Valley conjugation of the verb always sticks in my mmmemory.

Somehow the new bike was produced. I don't knnow if he told me to go over to the lush side garden, where I found it; whether he went there himself and theatrically wheeled it out to my amazement; or whether it was already there, leaning next to him on its stand, sparkling in the twilight, in plain sight as I approached with timidly accelerating steps. The bike was a more "adolescent" model: a manly deep red, a larger frame and flat brown seat that betrayed no hint of banana. I thanked him and felt happy, though there was also a sense, as has often happened with me before and since, of my not having earned this prize, especially after my previous insolent disobedience and deserved loss.

All that was forgotten, though, by him and me as I took the new bike (a little too big, awkward) for a spin on the street before his approving gaze. The truth was, I didn't really like this bike much. I've discovered that I can be stubbornly dissatisfied with replacements, even demonstrably superior ones, for things I've grown used to or fond of. I missed my dorky purple bike, despite the tougher, faster, cooler red one my father was so proud of, the present he had presumably bought somewhere up north and lugged back down for me, thinking the whole time how delighted it would make me. Or maybe he only bought it somewhere locally. I don't know.

The bike was definitely brand new, though — again, making it a more appropriate rite of passage prop than the cheap stolen banana hand-me-down I used to share with my sister. (Why was it stolen? Why did I let it be? Did I simply think it was such a useless-looking rickety piece of shit that nobody would bother lifting it, that only I could possibly care for it or bother with it and that this gave it a kind of immunity from theft?) Now none of that mattered. Dad smiled, his eyes narrowed to slits (I remembber the blazing, unprecedented openness of those crazed white orbs when boy-handling me and yelling at me before), and I rode smoothly away in a frictionless universe restored to its natural order.

The second epilogue is somehow more proper than the first, though without the first it couldn't have happened. About two weeks after I got it, the red bike — a youngster's gleaming metallic symbol of approaching manhood, bequeathed to him by his happy father — was ripped off too. This time it wasn't my fault. Not out of guilt or fear, but simply not wanting to upset my father again, I had consistently and conscientiously parked the thing in the back yard, like I'd been told. (Dad patiently reminded me on Grandma's driveway, now that I recall, to always keep it in the back.) The thieves took Big Red one night anyway, and I can't say I was all that disappointed. It was a little uncomfortable and I had built up no attachment to it. Dad, when he heard the news, was unmoved, like I'd expected him to be the first time. He must have had other things on his mind, or maybe he'd forgotten the whole bike business; as I've said, everything about it, from his extremes of emotion towards me to his magnanimous gift-giving — was really weirdly unusual. The second bike simply went the way of the first, we both pretty much just shrugged about it, and from then on I walked wherever I needed to go.

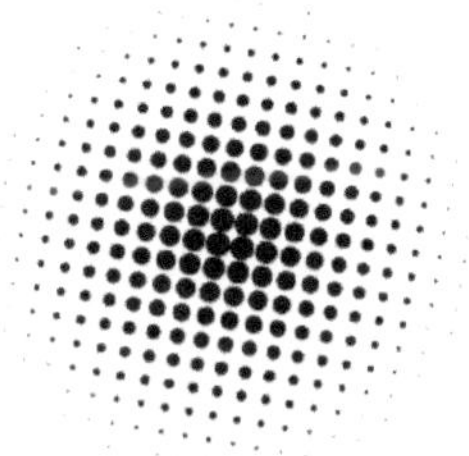

Sam

1986

Valley Youth Dead in Shooting Accident

EDINBURG — A 1986 high school honors graduate perished in an accidental shooting south of McCook Sunday.

Sam Huff, 18, of McCook, and some friends were shooting at cans at the ranch of a mutual friend when a sudden disturbance caused Steven Pawelek, 18, also of McCook, to turn suddenly just as his weapon discharged.

The .22 caliber rifle's bullet pierced Huff's heart and one lung.

An attempt to rush the youth to Edinburg General Hospital failed when the pick up truck he was being driven in broke down after its engine exploded. Huff was eventually taken to EGH by other county residents but was pronounced dead on arrival at the emergency room.

Funeral services will be held Tuesday at 10 a.m. at our Savior Lutheran Church in McAllen.

Edinburg High School records indicate that Huff was a member of of the National Honor Society and planned to attend Texas A&M University this fall as a freshman.

The Huff family suggests that memorial contributions be sent to the Sam Edward Huff Memorial Fund, care of the National Honor Society, EHS.

I wander in the big church parking lot.
Tony's white Monte Carlo is nowhere.
The day is hot with real Valley August stuff-your-nostrils hot.
Jesus, they're parked into the next block.
It is white. Tony's car is white. The day is white. Hot white. White hot. Hot. White. My head is one long throbbing explosion. I belch at a blue sedan. Sweating, squinting, I wander in the big church parking lot in a sea of metal looking for Tony's car. I can feel the bile rising.

The truck speeds along the flat highway, engine howling in agony. The fan belt spins, stretches, strains, heaves, lurches, pumping more more more. The engine is growing dizzy, its heart will burst. The hospital lies still five miles away.

"Seriously..."
"Seriously."
"To Sam."
"To Sam. Fuck, yeah."
(—CLINK—)
(gLuGgLUgGlUgGLUGGluGgLuggluGGlUGgLUg—ahhhhhhh)
(Joe and Mike in Mundo's apartment with its cheap Western furniture and nice stereo and terrifically-stocked fridge and bar and Mundo away at the island Monday night)
"Shit, man, I still don't..."

"WHAT?"

"Turn that shit down. I SAID, that I still don't believe he's, y'know, gone. Y'know? I mean, not in a sad way or anything, just in an intrinsic, empirical...whatdayacall it ... demonstrABLE ... DEmon ... deMONstrable way. Y'know. I cannot right now make myself believe that he couldn't right now walk through this door. I mean, I can't, man."

"I can. He wouldn't come through THIS door."

"Why?" (meaningful look from Mike, a sort of knowing smirk)

"Aw, come on. He knew about Mundo. He wouldn't've cared about that shit. He was a nice guy."

(Sam Hart was the nicest guy Joe had ever known in his life)

"SUCH a nice guy."

"Don't be an asshole."

(tremendous belch from Mike, the way only he can deliver 'em. and the night is young yet)

"Hey, man, I'm an instant asshole. Just add alcohol."

"You got that from a T-shirt. Fucking plagiarist. I'll get it for you when we're up in Austin."

(God it's good to be young. even when you don't realize it most of the time, it's good to be young and finished with high school and moving within the week up to college to live with your best friend and just feel how good it is because you know you're gonna live forever)

(just like him. two days ago, just like him)

Steven keeps the pedal down hard. His foot presses so hard to his boot to the accelerator that it hurts, tingles. His pudgy dirty hands grip the wheel so tight they absorb all the wheezing engine's throb. The muscles are taut. His eyes bulge out of the sockets and the whites strain out of his eyes. Everything is fast and bright and whirling by and the speed consumes all and yet, within that speed and noise and tingle all over his body, everything is in slow motion. Steven doesn't stop to think, "Just like in the movies."

I just couldn't take it in there any more, that's all. All the flowers and packed aisles and his family there in the front row and his cute litle sisters in pretty dresses and everyone with their backs to me through the glass partition at the very rear of the hall except for the orating priest before the coffin and my stomach in twisted knots and hell I gotta get outta here. Tony was late to pick us up and we had to stand at the back in the packed church. Even teachers he didn't have showed up for him, like Mrs. Hurtzwell, there in front with Francine. Of course, I see mainly anglos. Being a McGriffinite, it's only natural that mainly his own people would show up to his funeral. Puros gringos. Half the anglo population of the Valley must be here. It's a who's who of the white minority. Funny thing is, Sam was darker than most Mexicans I hang out with.

Of course, it could just be my condition. I can't concentrate on anything; it's all coming at me through a haze. This place is too cold. Sam's place is cold. Sam is...

I just had to get outta there.

The traffic is light. Cars make way at the sound of his wild , frantic honking. Something that horn screams scares them off. Sweat streams all over his fat red face. His freckles glisten. His eyes dart down, to the prostate form of his best friend, lying across the cab seat and Rene's lap, the head resting on his own knee, by the steering wheel. The engine is really shaking now, coming apart at the seams, howling as it goes. His best friend moans in a hollow voice that sets new tingles through Steve's body. Another car veers off in terror of what the horn says.

The horn screams murder.

"...EYES OF TEXAS ARE UPON YOU, ALL THE LIVE-LONG DAY..."

(disintegrates into laughter. Joe stands in the middle of the room on the dark blue carpet dancing a jig. Mike seems constantly coming and going from the kitchen with a new beer in his hand. it seems like a symphony of can tabs spluttering open)

"Hey, man, someone's at the door."

"Mundo! What're y'doin' here?"

"Ai, you all. What are you doing? Todos borachos estos pinches guercos sinvergüenzas, ai no."

"You're supposed to be ... where're you s'posed to be?"

"This is my friend Eddie."

"Hello. Mike's around here somewh ... Oh, wait, Mundo, wait. We were just singing ASS OF TEX ... I mean ..."

"Have you guys eaten everything already?"

"So you just graduated?"

"Yeah ... we haven't had too much yet."

(Eddie puts his arm around Joe. the older man's paunch presses against his waist)

"How old are you, Joe?"

"Eighteen."

"We're having a party back where I live. You want to come with us to the island?"

(Mike belches loudly)

"Oh, there you are. Where'd you go?"

"Bleedin' the monster."

"This is Eddie. Excuse me."

"Hi."

"'lo."

"Mundo, why did you come back? Don't trust us or something?"

"I just needed some things. You sure you wanna be doing this before the funeral tomorrow?"

"Yeah, yeah, no problem. I think Eddie likes me."

"Eddie likes everybody."

"Figures. He's a friend of YOURS."

"Ai, don't tread on me 'til you try me. I don't want you to eat these ... Mike, don't eat these, okay? I'm saving them for my mother. Don't eat them. Have whatever you want, but don't eat them. See, they even say Queen's cookies. Okay? They're the QUEEN'S cookies, okay? Don't eat them."

"Mundo, make me a scotch and tonic. Please please please please..."

"Ai, pepino. You're gonna feel like shit tomorrow."

"Sam won't mind."

A bird or something blocks the sun for a second. I'm lost in this damn parking lot. Naturally we were late, so naturally, we should be parked farther away, right? Goddammit. It occurs to me that I didn't call Mom last night. She doesn't know where I am, probably. The vodka taste is soaked into my gums. When I woke up this morning my mouth smelled a lot worse. I opened my eyes at the sound of something crashing down, and Mike says, "Shit!" I asked what the hell he was doing in the closet and he said he was looking for a tie. My head pounded so hard it felt like the bed was plopping up an down out in the middle of the ocean or something. Mike says, "Check this out, man," and I looked at it and it was a picture of two young boys doing something together and I asked what the hell is that and Mike says it's called NUT magazine. I told him he shouldn't be looking through other people's drawers. I asked if he'd called Tony and he says yes then goes back to grossing out over the magazine for what seems like a longer time than we probably have. But somehow my body won't move. My legs are made of fucking stone.

Tony's car shimmers painfully in the distance. I look both ways before I cross.

In the bed of the truck, bouncing and rattling, is a rifle. The spot where it was thrown shows a small dent. Sam groans, more weakly.

"Lemme do Hamlet. Lemme do...whoops."
(the room spins around, comes up to meet him, embrace him. it doesn't even hurt. Joe breathes in the lint and scum of the big blue carpet)
"Mundo ... Mundo ... Hey, man. Tell Mundo to c'mover here."
"They left a long time ago, man."
"Oh."
"Hey, man, that Eddie guy's a faggot."
"No shit ... What'd you expect?"
"It's disgusting. Damn, man. Get 'im away."
(Mike exists only as a disembodied voice, an occasional belch over the music. Joe strains and turns his head to make him real)
"...FALLING...OFF...THE RAILS...OF A CRAZY TRAIN..."
(half of the world is total black. the other half has Mike in Dutch angle dancing with a Bud in his hand before the stereo. he looks so funny jamming. happy. skinny asshole)

"Were not gonna make it, man," Rene says, "the engine's gonna die."
"SHUT UP! WE'LL MAKE IT!" Steven replies. Sam's black blood squirts out in rythymn from between his fingers like something out of a sewer pipe. Smoke shoots out of the hood, gets caught and stripped by the wind.

"Siddown, man. Siddown."
"What the fuck d'you want?"

"How much've you had?"

"I dunno."

"We gotta talk. This's serious. We gotta talk."

"Sure. What'sa matter?"

"We gotta talk."

"Yeah? What is it? You thinkin' 'bout Sam?"

"Nah, nah, not that. I'm not thinkin' 'bout Sam ... Well, maybe, in a way, yes."

"What? Shit, is THAT how much you've had, man?"

"It's still a quarter full. Or, an eighth. Or a third. Ah, I dunno. Look man, you an' me—this is SERIOUS SHIT—you an' me ..."

"Yeah?"

"... well, we been friends a long time, right?"

"Yeah, man, a long time ... shit, you're gonna die ..."

"I'M NOT GONNA DIE. We been friends a long time. We been through a lot. I don't even wanna think 'bout all the shit we've been through ..."

"Yeah."

"... and in a week we're gonna be living together ..."

"Uh-huh." (another belch)

"Livin' together. Y'unnerstan? LIVIN' TOGETHER."

"... As opposed to dying together."

"Das right. Das damn right. Damn yer good. We're gonna be living together. And before we do..."

"Yeah..."

"Before we do, we should know each other ..."

"Yeah, yeah ..."

"... so I want you to tell me what you think. I want you to tell me what you really really really REALLY think 'bout me. Tell me, man. Tell me what you really think. And I'll tell you what I think'a you. But you first. OKAY?"

"Yeah..."

"Tell me, goddammit. Don't spare me anything. This is SERIOUS SHIT. I want you to rip me open. Tell me the truth, man."

"Okay."

"Tell me the real fuckin' truth."

"Okay."

"Tell me what you really think about me."

"I will."

"I wan' the truth. You gonna tell me? You promise?"

"Yeah, I promise."

"Okay. So tell me. Right here, right now. Tell me. Tell me the truth. Okay? Okay. Let's hear it."

The engine explodes. White sparks fly off, swallowed by wind. A sickening metal sound —shards, shrapnel, shreds—kicks and kicks and rubs and scrapes under the hood. The steam and smoke cling closely to the truck as it slows, turning and grinding, and lurches off the road to a halt.

Steven's cries echo off the cows and crabgrass and mesquite. Sam has lost consciousness. Black wet shirt rags mingle with his guts. A metallic-sweet blood smell like alcohol spirits mixes with the humid air. The rifle has settled in a corner amidst a litter of bullets.

—o;ytrkIUW650tpq8kjio]ytr8kl98oih9IOYH87JHlk—"oh god ... oh god—

8947YGEF90==0OREUR7YKJ09w84kjsa0-7874287KJop'ew0— JESUS CHRIST, man ..."

"Hold on, man, hold on. Keep your head up."

"ouch...ouuuuch..."

"Come on, man. Here drink some water. Drink it."

"i can't...ouuuuuuuuuuuuuuuch..."

"Joe, god damn it..."

— I k j d s j o i H Y V [V 7 6 3 6 { J N U Y T j h y u 9 6 (I) O8YRTW96TYKItuewhu89KJSE8T—

"huh ... huh ... huh ...."

"Keep your head UP, man, GODDAMMIT ... Shit."

"ouch..." (forehead on cold white linoleum with slop the smell the smell)

"Here. Look up, LOOK UP. Christ, man. What a mess. I thought he told you not to eat those cookies ..."

"ouuuuuuuuuuuuuch ... i'm sorry, man ... ouuuuuuuch ..."

— U Y T L ; O ; G - = U I 3 7 8 I 1 R 4 W L K F G ,MUYouytd%&*#%wtrpre87925T342^*7—

"mike....miiiiiiiiiiiike...."

"What d'you want, man?"

"... hold my hand, man ... hold my hand ..."

Another car approaches, a cop siren moans, getting closer, but Steven knows it's too late. He and Rene pick him up, slap his face, carry him out of the cab. He's white; the sun's rays make him yellow. The world glows like an overexposed photograph. They'd known each other since they were kids. A thousand times they'd gone out shooting cans and bottles and jackrabbits. The next day they were going to A&M together, study agriculture and veterinary science. It was all set. Set in stone.

Sam is gone.

I stick my head out of the car window just in time for the pavement to catch my bile. That's all there is; I haven't eaten today. I lie back in Tony's rear seat with the door open, feeling a little better.

The Valley heat has a way of freezing everything; it just hangs there, kills the wind, stultifies, turns the world into a postcard where movement seems unnatural. As I settle into the seat, I blend into this motionless world. Eyes blocked against the glare, I breathe in the car smells: upholstery, cigarette ash, an old coke stain, various cans and trash on the floorboard. It seems my body has decided that sweating would be useless in this heat.

I'm gonna miss the burial. Dammit. I never knew him well. He was just this simple,

unassuming guy in one of my history classes, back when I didn't know how valuable "unassuming" could be. He wasn't particularly intelligent or interesting, but he was nice, sincerely nice. Nice is usually a bad word, but it wasn't with him. He gave being nice a good name.

He ran around with what was widely regarded as a hick crowd — Future Farmers of America, 4-H Club, Cow Raising Pig Shit Shoveling Club of America. I'd been on a farm maybe twice in my life, and didn't like it.

He made some pretty bad jokes. In my yearbook there's this picture of our class sitting out in the hallway for lecture because the school air conditioner had broken down. There he is, sitting next to me on the floor, his head bent forward and eyes shut. After we'd traded books to sign, I looked at that picture. Next to his slumbering self he'd written ZZZZZZZZZZZZZZZ.

We never went out together. Different circles. He ate in a different part of the cafeteria, he belonged to other student organizations, he sat far away somewhere at the football games. But he always had a kind word, and that always struck me. He was white, though so swarthy that you could have easily taken him for a Hispanic. I imagine he probably got some grief over that.

My fondest memory of him will always be that day in class when he stepped up in front of everybody to demonstrate lassoing skills. It was the week we were studying the King Ranch. Dressed in full cowboy regalia (I thought he looked silly but that was somehow okay for him), he showed us how to tie the rope and twirled it over his head and ours so widely that I thought there'd be an accident. He almost hit Jean Dunnemeyer when he lassoed an empty chair. He was damn good; he got it on the first try. The rope wrapped around that chair so pretty that it looked like one of those fast motion time-lapse films of a plant vine twining around a pole. We cheered, yahooed. He smiled and straightened his cowboy hat, and I saw sweat on his brow. Poor guy, he'd been nervous the whole time.

And here I am, hung over at his funeral.

I clear my throat, swallow a little bile mixed with saliva. Guess I've got a while; I haven't been to a church in ages but I imagine the service will last at least another half hour. I yawn, stretch, feel my rigid body popping —

And then I see him. Standing there, in the frame of the car door, faded jeans, white shirt, cowboy smile. The world is at its absolute most still, most silent.

Leaning up, I say, "Sam," like I was running into him in the hall in the morning or something. He grins, shows his teeth, his eyes laughing. Without thinking I look quickly down to his chest, all over his torso, but there's nothing—a clean immaculate white shirt. We sort of stare at each other for a minute as the world spins with both of us on it and then, as if by itself, my hand slowly reaches up to touch him. He stretches his own hand towards mine.

We touch. His image shimmers just like a highway mirage or ripples in a pond and there's this tiny instant where I see him last; he's smiling, his face says something friendly, something warm, like, "Thanks, man," or "Take it easy," or "Hope you're doin' okay," or "It's all right," and I blink and that's it.

Sam's gone.

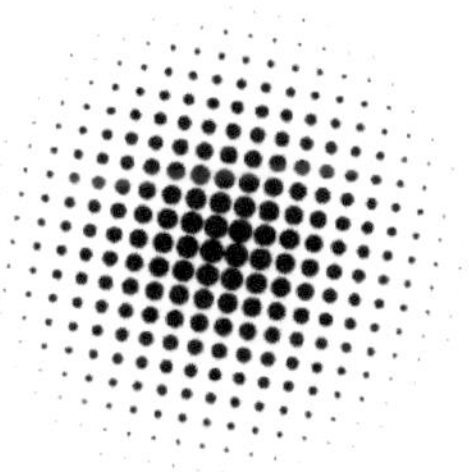

The Last Time

1994

The last time I spent any real time with him was in November, 1994, when he came to stay with me in LA for about 10 days. He spent three of those days in San Diego, giving a lecture on Russia at some university or other, but I hardly noticed he was gone. I had plenty of other things on my mind at the time, and besides, I'd ceased feeling his absence long before.

What happened over the course of that week in November, subdued and sad as it was for him, was nonetheless typical. Everything that Joe signified to me, every bad aspect of his that had driven me away over the course of our ten years "together," all that crappy attitude and obnoxious cockiness of his came out, the same as ever, even though to his credit (I suppose), for my sake (I suppose), he spent most of his time fighting those baser demons of his nature. But he couldn't keep them down for long. It would have been like asking an alcoholic to quit cold turkey.

I had gone through my spiritual and personal lifestyle changes over the course of almost two years — two years away from him. And here he was, pathetically, frantically, hopelessly trying to ape me and my thinking, trying to build bridges over too great an expanse, trying to make up for over a decade of abuse. He failed. And when he realized it was useless and he couldn't touch me anymore, he just sort of curled up into himself and walked around like someone had clipped his Green Lantern dick and when I bothered to notice his mood, I admit it: I was glad.

I knew he'd get over it. I knew his feelings, like everything else about him, were only temporary. But at that moment, after our last fight, when I saw him sitting despondently on the sofa in my living room, stroking our tabby

Ringo, I was gladdened by his disappointment, his sad dog expression. But, like I said, that was only when I bothered to notice it.

There are a few memorable things about his visit, not all of them bad. There might have been more of them, I guess, if not for his bad timing. He'd come right when I was really busy with my graduate scriptwriting program at school, and that was also around the time when I was getting together with Jaime, my first girlfriend at USC. Bad timing can ruin a lot of things, even in the best conditions, and I think that's part of what went wrong for him on this trip. I say for him, because for me ... well, by then I really couldn't care less.

We had a nice little moment early on. At that time I lived in a house overlooking Echo Park. It was a nice area, I liked it. Lots of Mexicanos. It actually reminded me a little of the Valley. We were driving by the park, and Joe looked out the window at the tall palm trees that line the pond. They're beautiful palms, longer and healthier than anything that grows in Aberdeen.

"You know what?" he said. "Those palms have the graceful curve of brontosaurus necks."

I smiled, a little puzzled, bemused. "That's a funny thing to say," I replied. "Can I use that?" It was good for a chuckle. Two writers, zipping along.

I remember on his third or fourth day here he was walking with me on my way to go edit a project he'd helped me film the day before. Joe had always liked to say he was apathetic about fashion, and that day his wardrobe choice was pretty bad. Imagine a 26-year-old man wearing a leather biker jacket with khaki pants, a blue sweatshirt and, worst of all, round-rimmed glasses. This, coupled with his pale skin and longish pony-tail, made me a little embarrassed to have him walking beside me.

Fashionably secure in my jeans and flannel, I smiled smugly as I said, "Look, Joe, if you don't want to invest in contacts, maybe you should think about wearing some other kind of jacket."

He turned to me, keeping stride, like I'd pointed out something totally alien to him. I had — or so he liked to pretend.

"You mean the two don't go together?" he asked.

"Of course not. You look ... I don't know."

"Geeky?" he offered.

" ... Yeah, I guess. But it's just wrong, more than anything else."

"Why?"

"It just is. I mean, if you're trying to go for this tough biker look and then bring in those glasses ... and those shoes ..."

"Wait a minute. Why do I have to 'go for' any look at all? Just for the sake of argument, why can't I dress how I want? Besides, I told you, I can't afford contacts right now and I didn't like 'em when I had 'em. Too much trouble."

I shook my head weakly, feeling more smug in the safety of my own good fashion sense.

"It's you, alright," I said. "It's you."

"What does that mean? 'It's you.' What the fuck is that?" But I could already see past that insouciant facade of his.

"Tell me something. Why do you wear that jacket?"

" ... Because I like it. It's black, I believe I look good in it. I'm a fall. It also keeps me warm, and I guess I've developed an attachment to it. Do you know this is the jacket I was wearing during the October events in Moscow?"

"So you wear it because you want to look good. You're concerned about your appearance."

"Well, not really. I mean ... okay ..."

"Why don't you just admit it?"

"Admit what?"

"That it bothers you. That what I pointed out about your clothes really bothers you. That you care about fashion."

"I don't care about fashion! Well, okay, no ... everybody cares about fashion, obviously."

"You want to fit in, like everybody else."

"That's right. That's right. Everybody has that feeling, that sense of wanting to fit in. I'm not saying I don't have it. I'm not saying I don't care about it. I'm just saying that I don't care about it enough to get a new jacket. I do care, just not enough, not as much as you and, I guess, the rest of the world. And as for contacts, I don't want any right now, even if I could afford them."

I smiled some more. "Like I said, it's you, alright."

We walked on, both of us realizing in our own way, that we'd slipped again into a conversation we'd been having, in one form or another, all our lives. Except this time I'd actually won, I'd gotten to him. I stole a glance at him and he was visibly disconcerted, even if it was just a little. Suddenly he pointed ahead.

"What about him?" he asked. "Is he wrong?"

Joe indicated a bald student type walking towards us on the sidewalk, wearing a black leather biker jacket, black leather boots — and blue shorts.

"Is the jacket and shorts thing in fashion yet? Does he look geeky?" Joe asked.

"Yes," I answered.

The guy passed by us with his friends. His nose was pierced.

"So that's a geek?" Joe pressed on.

"Well ... I'm only talking about his clothes. Yes, I think that looks wrong. But I'm not judging him as a person. It's a fashion judgment."

"Ah," Joe pointed his finger to the sky, "but as you were just trying to prove to me, fashion reflects on the person. Therefore, a fashion judgment is a person judgment, at least to some extent."

" ... Yes," I was forced to admit.

"And fashion is a real mutable thing. In 20 years they may be looking at what you wore and saying, 'Man, that looked so dorky.' So who can say what's geeky? Maybe glasses and shorts with leather jackets are the next big thing. Maybe me and my friend there are just ahead of our time."

"Well, I can't imagine that what you're talking about will ever be fashionable."

"Yeah, but if it is, you'll be walking the streets too, showing off your glasses and biker jacket along with everyone else."

"No, I don't think so. I wouldn't dress that way even if it was fashionable."

The talk ended there. It was a sort of draw. He'd lost the distressed look from his face, and I sensed he appreciated the constructive criticism. At least it meant I was giving him attention, however briefly. We walked on, both still secure in our beliefs. Me probably more so.

But that was a more tame Joe, by then. What I remember most vividly about his time here (and if he were alive he'd probably be hurt that I choose to focus on this) is the dinner we had with my roommate Jan his first night in LA.

We'd just gotten out of lecture (we'd gone there straight from the airport), and he asked for an Indian restaurant, because there "isn't any Indian food within 200 miles of the Valley!" He'd been staying with his sister in Aberdeen for over two months, and he really missed Indian cooking.

Jan agreed wholeheartedly, and I was more or less neutral, thinking I could probably find something at an Indian restaurant that would comply with my diet. So, we went to this place called Siva and he was thrilled, kept saying how one of the girls he'd dated in Moscow was called Siva, which I knew, but Jan was interested in.

"And her brother was called — guess what — Vishnu," he said, trying to charm her, I could tell.

Jan, like me, like virtually everybody I'd met my first semester at USC, was an aspiring screenwriter. Ambitious, easygoing, a Leo. She'd moved out to the city 10 years before, after 20 years in Indiana. She'd driven here in her '82 Toyota Celica with her tabby, Ringo, lying across her lap the whole way.

The evening was going alright, though already I was feeling my old sense of dread — justified or not. Going out with Joe was like walking a minefield; you never knew what obnoxious thing he was going to say next, what embarrassing fact about you he was going to dredge up in front of strangers. Madeleine, his ex-girlfriend, and I were in total agreement on that one. Joe was a total loose cannon in conversation. No appreciation whatsoever for the feelings of others. Sure, later on he'd claim surprise that you were actually bothered by what he'd said; it was all just harmless space-filler to him. His saying that would only piss you off even more.

Well, however promising that dinner with Jan had begun (and it hadn't, not very), it turned into a vintage Joe performance.

We started by discussing my macrobiotic diet, what I could and couldn't eat, what circumstances led me to choose macro as my lifestyle, and why, after two years of feeling healthy and happy with my body, I would never go back to my old eating habits.

Joe had heard all this before and chewed his deep-fried appetizer, waiting for me to finish. When I mentioned that macro had helped me shed 30 pounds, Joe chimed in with his usual sensitivity, "Yeah, he wanted to be called Roy Batty, but we used to call him Roy Tubby."

As Jan and Joe laughed, my roommate noticed that I wasn't joining them, but my former best friend, true to form, didn't bother to look. Poor Jan. All that week, she was in the unenviable role of witness to a dead friendship, rotting slowly right in her own house. Good material for a scriptwriter, I guess, once you get over that "slow train wreck" feeling.

The talk went on, and Jan eventually asked me how Joe and I had met. I cringed. That devilish glint came to Joe's eye. He turned to me, smiling, and asked that same, age-old question he'd asked me at countless other such occasions.

"You want to tell it, or should I?"

It wasn't so much a question, really, as the opening line of the performance. Joe certainly never let me answer. Almost immediately he'd say, as he did now, "Okay, I'll tell it."

And away he went.

"It's actually a pretty cool story. It's cool because it happened when we were just kids, because it tells a lot about our characters and the way we would develop as friends later on, and because it involves someone else we'd get to know. Roy and I met at a fifth-grade short story contest."

"Yeah, but that wasn't really when we met as friends," I interrupted, trying desperately to derail the damn thing. "We met for real in high school, in class ..."

"Yeah, yeah," he said. "But this was when we had our first real clash, when we first crossed swords, and it's a funny story. It's apocryphal. You wanna hear this, don't you, Jan?"

She hesitated a little, but of course she knew nothing about any of this, about us. To her it was just a story, one Joe seemed eager to tell.

"Sure," Jan said. "Go ahead." I settled back, dug in.

"Okay. Like I said, this was in fifth grade. Now, I didn't know Roy personally at the time, right. We went to different elementary schools. I was at Stephen F. Austin and he was at ... what was your school called?"

"Travis," I said, on cue.

"Travis. Right. So we didn't know each other. But I'd heard about Roy, see. I'd heard about him. I was like, the class brain at my school, though I was still really popular. Back then, not later. Anyway, I'd been hearing, y'know, here and there about this other guy at Travis elementary, who was supposed to be really smart, and everybody said he was just like me."

"Wow," Jan said.

"Yeah. So I was, like, intrigued by him, even before I'd met him, I was intrigued. So I kept my eye out for him. Well, before long, we had this contest at my school for the best short story, and I won. So I got to go and compete on the district level, with the other schools. Okay. So, guess where the district contest is held. Travis elementary. And guess who's competing from Travis in the contest. Roy. That's right. Roy Tubby. And someone else also came to that competition, someone that we would get to know later. Eva. It was so cool. It was, like, baby Roy and baby Joey, and baby Evie. Like, when they show you some famous character when he was young? Like Muppet Babies? Like, have you seen *Indiana Jones and the Last Crusade,* where they have River Phoenix as teen Indie? Well, this was exactly the same thing. Exactly. It was a prologue to greater things, and like all prologues, it contained the seeds of everything that would come later. It contained the future in embryonic form ..."

"Tell the story, Joe," I said, a little too curtly. He was really dragging it out this time.

"Alright. So, it's me and Roy and Evie, all gathered in this room with, I don't know, ten other kids. We don't know each other at all, except when they announce Roy's name as one of the contestants, and right away I'm paying attention. I got a good look at him. Now, what people don't appreciate is how different Roy looked as a kid. He was, you know, chubby. And he wore these super-thick Coke-bottle glasses and he had an afro, or it looked like an afro. His hair was really curly and black, like Gene Shalit. Actually, it looked that way even in high school ..."

"Joe ..." He was doing it again. Like countless times before. I was losing it.

"Okay, okay. Relax. Okay, so I got a good look at him and I'm, like, shitting my pants. I mean, he looked really intelligent. Nerdy and intelligent. I mean, I wasn't the coolest-looking kid either, but this kid ... I mean, total Mr. Brainiac. Okay. So there we are, and the contest begins.

"It works like this. This wasn't, like, a complete short story you had to write."

"I was gonna say," Jan said.

"Yeah, we would've been there all night. So what they did was give you the beginning of a story, just a simple little story, a couple of characters, and then you're supposed to finish it, give it a good ending based on what they've given you. We were just, whatever, ten-year old kids or whatever. Fifth graders. So they give us the beginning of the story, and then you have an hour to finish it.

"Okay. So this is the story they give us. The beginning of it. This was around the time of *Star Wars,* by the way, so they give us this science fiction-based story. Went like this. Uh ... a couple'a kids, little Timmy and Janie or whatever, are walking home late at night after a showing of *Star Wars.* It's really dark and they're walking through this unfamiliar part of town, behind a fence or something. And it's really dark, right, so Timmy and Janie have their battery-operated light sabers out, like flashlights. I remember that was funny, 'cause I had one of those when I was a kid. They were cool. Alright, so they're walking late at night and they're talking about the movie and how great it was, and how cool it would be to meet aliens from another planet.

"All of a sudden, Timmy and Janie look up, and what do they see but a mysterious, glowing object in the sky flying slowly towards them. A flying saucer. And that's it. That's all they gave us. We were supposed to take the story from there and finish it. So, we start writing. We have an hour.

"Well, it was a pretty tense time for me, 'cause I really wanted to win. But one look at Roy and I knew I was up against someone good, someone who could beat me. I didn't give a shit about any other kid in the room, but Roy scared the crap outta me. And, as the minutes tick by, I realize I'm spending all my time looking at him, across the room. We all sat around thinking about what we were going to write, and one by one the kids lowered their heads and started to scrawl their endings onto their sheets of paper. Roy started writing after only about two minutes.

"But I was just getting more and more nervous. Finally I tore myself away from watching him write and started thinking about my story. The flying saucer was going to land, okay, I knew that. It would land in front of Timmy and Janie in a secluded field behind the fence. It was so late that no one else would see it but the children. And then ... and then ... hmm. I had to think hard on this. Above all I wanted to avoid cliché. I'd seen plenty of sci-fi movies where the ship lands and aliens come out and say ... hmmm. And that's when an idea came to me.

"The saucer would land, this strange octagonal door would blossom open, and out would step this humanoid creature in a silvery suit. It would raise its three-fingered hand and say, in a deep commanding voice, 'I am not the first and I am not the last. I have come to your planet to help you in this time of great problems ... blah blah blah. That was the story. A benevolent alien comes to Earth to help in our age of crisis, and he chooses two children to help him understand the human race, and they eagerly take up their role, guiding him through his first tentative steps in interplanetary interpersonal relations. At the end the kids introduce the alien to the president of the United States. They live happily ever after.

"That was my story. In the middle of writing it, I look up at the clock, and I see that about 20 minutes have ticked off, and I've got about a page, so I'm making good time. I'm confident with my piece, and I'm enjoying the writing of it, when I happen to look over at Roy again. And then my confidence crumbles. I see that he's already starting his third page, and he looks really ... well, like he's really concentrating. He's scribbling away like mad, oblivious to everything around him, he's even got his tongue on his lip like Charlie Brown writing a pen pal letter.

"'Damn!' I thought. 'His story is probably a lot better than mine. He's obviously really enthusiastic about it. Shit!' I took a look at what I'd written and it seemed like the most generic, clichéd pap anybody had ever regurgitated onto paper. It sucked. It was like *The Day the Earth Stood Still* meets Walt Disney. Totally worthless. Well, now I was really in trouble. Roy was writing away like Ray fucking Bradbury, and I had a total dud on my desk. In total shock, I decided to scrap my first idea and come up with something more original. I had to win this contest. I had to beat this guy.

"The clock was ticking like a time bomb ready to explode in my face. I saw I had only 25 minutes left when I started frantically writing my second idea. It had taken me that long, in the panic I was in, to come up with what I thought was a good, original story.

"Now the flying saucer crashed-landed into the fence. But the ship emitted this powerful magnetic field which negated any sound, so that the crash was completely silent. Unfortunately, the ship also crashes right into little Janie, killing her on impact. Timmy, overcome with grief, rips open the octagonal door and in a rage he storms into the ship, his light saber poised to strike at his friend's murderers.

"He finds, to his surprise, a roomful of small furry pink creatures, with antennae and a single glowing horn emanating from the top of their heads. Timmy notices immediately that most of the creatures are not moving, their horns are barely glowing, like they're too weak to defend themselves against the intruder. 'What are you things?' he screams at them. 'Why did you kill my best friend?'

"'Please don't hurt us!' Timmy hears inside his mind. The creatures are telepathic. 'We meant no harm!' The lead alien, whose name is Tal Orl'an, explains to Timmy that he and his companions are desperately ill. They've traveled the galaxy in search of a cure for their illness, which has affected their entire planet. This ship is a peaceful research vessel, manned by scientists. Their onboard computer, which ran the ship while the crew was in cryogenic stasis, guided them to Earth. But the ship was struck by a meteorite while entering orbit and Tal Orl'an had to try and land the ship manually, and a crash-landing was the best he could manage. Now the aliens were begging for Timmy's help.

"'But you killed Janie!' Timmy said. 'How I can help you with your illness if you've murdered my best friend?' Tal Orl'an is surprised. 'Oh my!' he says. 'Did I land on someone? Tell me, quickly, did you hear anything when the ship crashed?'

"'Actually, no,' Timmy answers. 'It was totally silent.' 'Thank X'orzz!' the alien exclaims. 'Then our magnetic field was not damaged by the meteor.

That means your friend was shielded from the impact and should be lying comfortably beneath us right now!' And so she was. Janie was fine. Once they get her out from beneath the ship, the aliens discover that Janie and Timmy have exactly the nutrient in their bodies to cure their sickness. Tal Orl'an explains that the children's contact with the ship's radiation has mutated their body chemistry so that now they're living reservoirs of precisely the medicine the aliens need to survive.

"But Timmy and Janie protest that they can't come with the aliens to save their planet. They don't want to leave their families. But they don't have to, Tal explains. The aliens only require a small dosage from them, and then they can synthesize the medicine. So the alien scientists remove Timmy's tonsils and Janie's appendix, both of which he says would have given the children complications any day now.

"The aliens repair the wooden fence with a 'reverse entropy' ray, and the kids help them patch up the ship. Soon they're all done and the aliens are about to leave. Janie asks the aliens — because Timmy won't be able to talk for a while after his operation — why they chose this particular town, at this particular time to show up. 'Oh, that's simple,' Tal Orl'an says, as his horn glows brighter. 'We saw your glowing sticks from orbit, and hoped they meant you were creatures like us, who would help us in our plight.' The children smile and flick on their light sabers.

The ship takes off, the aliens are saved, and Timmy and Janie have some new friends who've left them a wonderful gift: a device that turns nuclear waste into delicious chocolate. The end."

"That's some story," Jan said.

"Yeah, and I had to write all that shit down in half an hour! I barely made it. I was with the last group of kids in the room. But even in my panic to write I noticed Roy had been one of the first ones to turn in his story and leave the room. And by the way, Eva was also one of us who stayed 'til time ran out.

"Well, we turned over our stuff, and it took the judges about an hour to grade 'em and pick the winners. I remember I saw Eva drawing horses on her notebook to pass the time, and I told her I liked how she drew. She said thank you. But I didn't talk to Roy at all. I was so strung out about this whole contest that I couldn't face him. So I stayed away and bit my nails nervously, waiting for the results.

"Finally they called us all back in. Roy had won first place, I won second place, and Eva won third. As a treat for the group, in addition to ribbons the winners got to read their endings out loud. Roy walked up in front of everybody, ready to read. I sat there, totally defeated. I had given it my best shot, and this guy had beaten me. What could he have written that was so original and fantastic that the judges chose his story over mine? I was about to find out."

He looked up to Jan. "Can you guess what it was that Roy wrote, what he won with?"

"I think so," she said.

"Well?"

"Does it happen to start with, 'I am not the first and I am not the last'?"

"Exactly. Exactamundo. Shithead here goes up in front of the whole group of kids and teachers and starts reading exactly the idea, exactly the same fucking dialogue, that I had written first, then discarded as too clichéd. The saucer lands. A humanoid creature in a silvery suit steps out, holds up his two-fingered hand and proclaims, 'I am not the first and I am not the last.' He's here to help in this 'time of crisis.' At first the humans hate him, but soon, with the children's help, they grow to accept him and his gifts of peace. Timmy and Janie help the creature understand human nature and he takes them and their families on a tour of the world. He brings world peace to the planet and prepares us for an attack from another alien race, a hostile one. They successfully defend themselves against the threat and a new age of brotherly cooperation dawns. At the end Timmy and Janie introduce the alien to the president of the United Nations.

"Jeesus fuckin' Christ! So, anyway, that was that. I got to read my story, which those judges had passed over in favor of something more ... familiar, shall we say, and then Eva read hers. Hers was actually pretty cool. In hers the ship belongs not to aliens, but to this group of technologically advanced women who live on a secret island in the middle of the ocean. The leader tells Timmy and Janie that they're fated to die on this night, the unfortunate victims of an earthquake. But the women will be happy to adopt them and raise them on the island, and later on reintroduce them into the world as adults, to help improve human — especially male-female — relations with the special training they'll receive. The earthquake starts, and the kids jump aboard. There was something else to it, some kind of twist at the end, but I've forgotten. Do you remember?"

"No," I answered him.

"Anyway, so that's our apocryphal 'origin' story. We didn't really get together until later, in the eighth grade, but I like to think of that as our auspicious meeting."

"Yeah," Jan said. "But why do you call it 'apocryphal'?"

"Oh, you know, apocryphal in the sense that nobody really knows exactly how the story went. I've probably embellished it a little here and there ..."

"Too much, if you ask me," I told him.

" ... but those are basically the facts of the story. Like I said, it tells a lot about how we would relate to each other in the future. At least, I like to think so."

Dinner went on from there. Jan did seem to enjoy the story, and Joe had recited it with his usual relish, as well as his usual lack of caring how I felt about it.

Later on, close to the time he was about to leave for home, when a whole week of disappointment in the state of our friendship had drained him of his normal vitality, we were on our way to meet Jaime, my new girlfriend, for dinner at a Thai place.

In the car I told Joe I didn't want any embarrassing anecdotes, no "short story contest" bullshit. I told him I was uncomfortable just having him around, and he better not humiliate me in public again.

With his long face, he nodded. That night he behaved like a dog on a short leash. He wasn't very entertaining, but he wasn't too much of an asshole, either. And that was all I wanted.

What Joe could never understand, you see, is that his "contest" story wasn't indicative of how we would "relate to each other in the future." It held no embryonic seeds of anything but his own delusion.

What was indicative — for me, painfully indicative — of how we used to behave together was the way in which he would go about telling that story. Launching into it without even stopping to think that the way he told it might put me in a bad light, mocking me at every turn, using me as a scapegoat to salve his bruised ego. Whenever I brought this up, he would go straight into denial.

"Come o-o-o-on," he would say. "You think I tell that story to, what, punish you or something? Do you honestly, really think that I would hold a grudge about some piddly little short story contest that happened in elementary school (fill in the blank) years ago? You think I'm that petty?"

By that fall of 1994, I was able to hold my ground, not give way to his denial, look him in the eye, and say, "Yes."

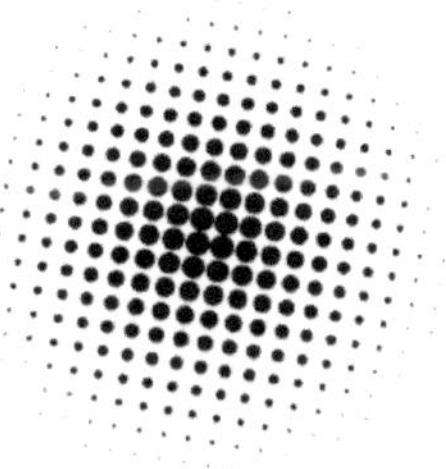

Faccia Prima

1997

As, at last, as his tongue swoops down on Tonya's clitoris, the first thought (as her moans begin in earnest) (as her pale body breathes a sigh and slackens) (as it slowly starts building myotonic tension and settles back onto the bed), the first inkling, sì, sì, sì, the first, the only resolution, tion, tion, the first thing he thinks, inks, inks, silently, to himself, self, the first thing he thinks, is: "I won't, won't, won't, stop, stop, stop, 'til, she's, there," — yes, so, it begins: ignition, venous dilation, tongue working smoothly on its springs, a hot young colt, tendons tight, lungs full, jaws flexed, hairy naked white body kneeling — oh, didn't call Mom — an oiled-dipped drill with one mission, catch, release, catch, release, tension, jerk, tension, jerk, a single, monolithic purpose, pale torso aimed, setter-like, focused, on the tiny point below her mons, stirring in its swaddling hood, her magnificent little third nipple, his only goal — a quick glance at the clock, "Starting incision, 12:59" — his only business, there, at the opening, at the source, of it all, at her slowly congesting, stiffening, wakening glans, is to service, service, service, sì, sì, service with a smile, sì, così, like that, like that, keep on, and so, on cue, on call, the first haul of saliva descends on Bartholi's steamy glade, a warm summer shower cascading, beading its dark whorly crown, trickling to the fecund soil beneath, where flowers sprout from their seeds with impatience, ducts tremble and open, open, open,

where two rivers meet, redouble, a dam slowly bursts, a waterfall bubbles, and things start to get slippery — so the fingers, the fingers dole out their aid, aid, aid, those apish digits, unbelieving, flattered, wowingly beside themselves with the honor, add their voices to the steadily mounting chorus, the polyphony of pressures on this one sacred spot, spot, ot, ot, here, here, here, here, *a este milagro,* this dainty dollop smaller than his pinkynail, this happy little grub named and unnameable that purrs beneath his wet, frictionless slide, slide, slide, slide, glis, san, do, this Darwinian magnum opus, us, a million-year recipe's tart 'n' tangy fruit, a thousand thousand thousand years all leading to this night and this man and this woman in this dark, disheveled room, towel on floor, clock on desk, window curtained, door locked, one man and one woman who writhe beneath the gaze of a grinning chrome grill, a roused 'lectric heater bathing her in soft orange light, watt-drenched rods burning, glowing, throbbing, scopophiliac facemask gazing, gazing not wavering an inch, not missing a stroke, and meanwhile he thinks, thinks — fingers slipping from their buttery perch, no, keep on, keep on — he thinks, draws back and inhales her hot, pungent aura, her jungle ripe, fertile, deep, one quick breath when his shadow pounces on the wall and the thin light finds her glistening pea, and the heater flares, saluting, gratified, and he suddenly thinks, sinks back into her, he thinks, he thinks, he thinks, oh, shit is my beeper off? and carries on his task, his sacred glossolalia, more mechanical now, distracted, stracted, adjusting his knees, craning his neck, bobbing up and down, a stubborn oil rig, and his mind swims back to his beeper, lying on the chair 'neath trousers tie the hurriedly cast-off sweater, nearby, the little bomb just waiting to burst, the tiny terrorist, poised to sabotage, the attendant nurse scheming to rob him, to rob them both, so I've got to think, think, think, did I? did I? did I turn the damn thing off? think, think, sì, così, così, keep on like that, oh God (her accent's musical mixture of British and Italian), and he thinks, thinks, keeping on, and then another thought while another flood seeps into and onto and around her nooks and crannies, left, left, right, right, pace picking up, nervously, up, up, up, up, up, loosing his breath, overflow dribbling down chin — "Wipe, please" — and, quickly, quickly rubbing it on her thigh, nervously, he can't put it off anymore, nervously, he snatches a chiaroscuro glimpse of her: the jutting rib cage; the faint seam — linea alba — where her two halves meet, sternum to pubic bone; the pink cupola breasts; and finally, finally, critically, yes, the face, the face, Which is it? yes, it's her face, the face, faccia prima: the roman nose, the thin lips half-parted, the large brown eyes swimming 'neath their lids, the gentle brows, the fair forehead, all set in a white oval itself resting in a pillow of long dark curls; it's her, it's her, yes, it's her, and, slipping, slipping back down for another sortie, reassured, he still asks, asks, sì, sì, sì, afraid of the question, sì, keep on like that, afraid of the answer, he still asks, he asks, he asks, "Who are you?" and

he's in the airport, an overcast day spilling in through the skylight, the hot crowd jostles 'round, over an hour standing here, an international flight, the passengers trickle out of the gate one by one, in slow intervals, freshly-hatched tortoises with stamped visas, scrambling to the sea, they push their luggage carts, sleepy, a ten-hour flight, and still she's not there, and the minutes drag on, more and more minutes piled onto their six months apart, and he begins to wonder, as the hugs and explosions of Italian erupt through the crowd, that maybe ... that maybe ... and suddenly someone is waving to him, a blonde woman pushing her cart as the auto-doors seal behind her, she's waving and her blue eyes sparkle and her white teeth shine and her head tilts in rapture, her bob swaying after it and I'm thinking, "It's a mistake," but she keeps walking right over to me, smiling, she's beautiful, but it's a mistake, but she's in front of me and she spreads her arms and joyously says, "Oh, I don't believe it," and I say, "Um, excuse, me, but ..." but she's already embracing me, holding me close, full breasts straining through her silk shirt against my chest, and she's saying, ecstatically, through a laugh, "Oh, God, I'd forgotten your smell," and I smell her too and she smells wonderful, her hair caressing my cheek, but I sort of wince and say, "Miss, uh, miss," and she's already trying to plant a kiss on me, those full lips, hungry lips, with the tip of her tongue just jutting out between them, and I say, a little too loud, "Miss, there's been a mistake," and I push her away, a little too hard, and the crowd keeps moving and bumping into us and as I guide her over to the railing I'm saying, "I think you've got me confused with someone else," and she says, "What are you talking about?" "I'm ... I'm not the person you're supposed to be meeting —" "What are you saying? What's the matter with you?" "Look, miss, I'm telling you, I mean, I don't know, but you've made a mistake ... Look, who are you supposed to meet?" and she tells me my name, and ... and ... and I ask her her name and she says Tonya, with a growing frown, and she tells me to stop playing games and I say I don't understand, and then I stare at her a second, she looks lost, and then I say,

"O-o-okay, this is a joke, right? She set you up for this? Come on, where is she? Is she watching or something?" "What the hell are you talking about?" and she's getting more and more alarmed and more and more offended, and a little Asian boy in a 49ers cap is staring at us and there's sweat on my brow and I ask her how the hell she knows my name and who is she and what's this all about and this isn't funny and she says, in a more and more irritated voice, that she's Tonya, "Your girlfriend, remember? From Milan? We've been seeing each other for two years? We've been talking on the phone for five months?" and she has no accent and then she starts telling me, looking me in the eye, she tells me who I am, that I'm a medical student, that I just finished my first year of rotations (and then she names my hospital), that my parents are divorced, that my mother used to live in Guanajuato but now she lives in Hawaii, that I have one brother, no pets, an apartment in the Mission, then she tells me my address, my phone number, the kind of computer I own, the speed of my modem, she tells me my favorite movies, my favorite authors, my blood type, my ring size, my social security number, my entire fucking sexual history and it's all true, every word, and she tells me that I spoke with Tonya just minutes before her flight took off, that she called me from Linate just to say she loved me and that's true too and all I can finally blabber is, "Wha ... I ... I don't ..." and the blonde woman's face is full of concern, her anger fading because she sees I'm not kidding — just as Tonya would see — and she squeezes my shoulder, and says, "It's alright, it's alright," and I insist, insist, that we check with the airline people and I look frantically around for Tonya in the thinning crowd, the automatic doors no longer open in the interlude between flights, and the counterperson, a gray-haired black man in a brown jacket, says that Tonya went through customs and the blonde woman shows both me and him her ticket, with Tonya's name on it, and the numbers all match, and I make her show us her passport and it says Tonya's name too and all the info is correct — but the photo, the photo is of this blonde woman, and the counterperson starts to shuffle and clear his throat and I catch Tonya ... no, the blonde woman, smiling apologetically and he says is there anything else he can help us with and, staring at the carpet, I let the woman lead me away, and this goes on for the next three hours, I demand that they let me into the customs area so I can look for Tonya, but they tell me, everybody tells me, that she's standing right here next to me and I wind up yelling at them and at her, but she doesn't get angry, she instead tries to calm me, comfort me — just as Tonya would — and she ends up driving me home, telling me more exact details about myself, recalling intimate conversations between me and Tonya, things only the two of us know — but the way she drives: she doesn't drive like Tonya, but at the same time, she knows where everything is in the car and she points at the picture on the dashboard and says, "You've still got that one, huh?"; she means the picture of me and Tonya in the Piazza St. Marco with a pigeon eating out of Tonya's hand, and I look quickly where she's pointing and my blood turns to ice when I see the picture, rattling softly with the motion of the car: the picture shows me and the blonde woman in the Piazza St. Marco, with a pigeon eating out of the blonde woman's hand; then I jump as my beeper goes off, it's not the hospital, and she takes the thing from my hand, gently, decisively, and says, "I'll call in sick for you," and soon she's pulling into my driveway, and when the car stops, she turns the beeper off and —

yes, yes, the beeper is off, she — *she, the other one* — she turned it off, yesterday, when they got home, in the car, he'd forgotten; too many other things on his mind, ind, ind, ind, sì, sì, sì, sì, oh, keep on like that, like that, please, up, up, up, vas, vas, vasocongestion, labia minora gently throb, throb, throb, folds of fleshy, glowing, pinkish-red lava, he can see it, see it, her vulval cynosure, her blooming, redolent bouquet, sì, sì, keep, on, keeeep, on, while amid the gurgles, the smacks, the loving soppy noises it flickers, his toadying tongue, a wet newborn mole, burrowing, furrowing, tunneling into its den, den, den — yes there — den — yes there, oh God — den, den, den, dart, dart, dar-ting, dart-ing, dart-ing, dance-ing, bounce-ing, pounce-ing, trounce-ing, ecco, ecco, ecco, ecco, yes-o, yes-o, yes-o, good-o, great-o, right-o, night-o, nipple, ripple, rupple, supple, suckle, sìckle, ruckle, rìckle, tickle, nickel, pickle, purple, circle, jerkle, jiggle, niggle, fickle, chickle, uncle, prickle, peter, piper, picked-a, peck'a, pickled, pepper, leper, lipo, fido, fuddle, fuckle, tuckle, knuckle, suckle, buckle, ruckle, den, den, den ... den ... en ... no, keep on, en, keep on, and he draws a gasping breath, forehead on her bush, bowing, bowing, tongue-tied, lips unnumbing, shake it out, shake it out, the glossitis, the fatigue poisons, shit, bowing, contrite, rueful, bowing, paganish, before his hot split-strawberry goddess, bowing, holding her open with his paws, pitiful, breathing in the mix of her anointment and his aftershave, and the flood of names, and charts, and morphologies — the clock glows 1:23 — and lectures, and metaphors, they're useless, useless to him now, and his thoughts float to airports, love, women, changes, dead — no, not dead, alove ... alive ... while he sees, in the rose-light, how her angry clit tumesceses, rumbles, her pissed-off little Aetna, and all he can do is lap it, lightly, lightly, and, shuddering, he begins again, gain, gain, takes a hot breath, releases, eases, eases, as fresh waves batter her craggy shores, and her bluff leaps, eaps, eaps, link remade, circuit fixed, nexus, vibrating, stiffening: tuning fork, antennae, lighting rod for orgone energy,[5] seeking more signal, more signal, more signal, signal, sì, sì, sì,

---

[5]While Doctor Wilhelm Reich's theories of "orgone energy" — a primal cosmic force that humans could tap through orgasmic release — have been widely discredited, this is not to downplay the profound mystery that orgasm, especially female orgasm, still represents for the medical community, as widespread and continuing research demonstrates; the mystery revolves around the clitoris, a unique organ, which, in stark contrast to all other structures of the human body, carries out no practical function, but rather seems designed for no other purpose than the receiving and transmittal of pleasure signals to the brain, thereby amounting to a bit of an evolutionary puzzle (or marvel); while some have theorized that the intense uterine contractions which accompany orgasm — three to fifteen contractions of the orgasmic platform with an initial three to six contractions at 4/5 second intervals, along with contractions of the external rectal sphincter at 4/5 second intervals — serve to flush semen deeper into the woman's body to facilitate sperm/ovum contact, this reasoning is questionable at best, there being no guarantee that the woman would ever achieve orgasm through simple vaginal intercourse (most women respond much more favorably to clitoral stimulation); to illustrate the variety of opinion regarding the "purpose" of female orgasm, we represent the following speculations: 1) the woman's climax serves to "enhance interpersonal bonding and promote monogamy" (Beatrix Hamburg, though critics point out that orgasm could just as easily encourage women to have more sex with more partners and toss monogamy out the window); 2) what might be called the afterglow" theory has it that the prolonged period a woman spends in a horizontal position after orgasm, like her uterine contractions, enhances the motility of the sperm to the eggs, though evidence for this hypothesis is scant; 3) finally, some psychologists posit that female orgasm is merely the accidental evolutionary analog to the male variety (cf. non-functioning nipples in men), and even go so far as to say that women's multiple orgasms (an ability which men, by and large, do not share) "may be an incidental effect of their inability to ejaculate" (sic); whatever the reason for female orgasm, its non-somatic effects are clear: the sudden release of beta enkephalins and fragments of endorphins into the body, stimulation of the hypotholamus and other pleasure centers in the brain, with correspondent sensations of well-being and a near-mystical euphoria, all the more rewarding in women since virtually all data since Tiresias show that a happy clitoris, uniquely designed to tap into pleasure (Dr. Reich's "orgone energy") is capable of producing orgasms of a depth, breadth, length and power unattainable and unimaginable by men ... now, thank you very much, ladies and gentlemen, but that's enough of this because I've got to get Tonya off ...

no, wait, that's wrong, that's wrong, the beeper, it's on, it's on, dammit, signal, signal, I think, remember? she was ... she was ... the blonde woman ... Tonya ... she was telling me over dinner, dinner at my place, she had made me take a shower to calm down, my shirt felt crisp and airy and tingly, like shirts feel after a shower — the shirt Tonya bought me, that I'd worn to meet her at the airport — she'd made a risotto dish, it steamed in the candlelight as we clinked wine glasses, it tasted like it always tasted when she made it, and she was telling me over dinner, the blonde woman, she was telling me that she'd called the hospital and they said I had the weekend off and she flashes those perfect teeth and her blue eyes bore into me, irises contracting, she's changed into one of my shirts and her bra dangles from my doorknob and her bags sit in a corner and I tell her, looking away, that I should keep the beeper on anyway just in case, and as I flick it on I feel numb, deadened, I've stopped reacting after I've dug through my pile of photos and this woman is in all of them, in Tonya's poses; after she smiles back at me, grotesque, bob frozen mid-swing, from the street artist caricature I asked her, Tonya, to pose for in Turin, the one tacked on my wall; after I hear the blonde woman's voice when I replay Tonya's last message on my machine; after she plucks from her bosom — nipples pressing the pinstripes, bars sine-curving tight about the breasts — she takes out the chain pendant that says *Ti Amo* with my name that I gave her, that I gave Tonya, for her 26th birthday; I've stopped reacting, by then I've stopped caring, except this woman, this virus, she's taking Tonya away, she's taking every last bit of her, where is she? what does she look like? what is (her) voice, (her) taste, (her) smell? (her) face? this woman is laughing, telling me something that happened with her sister, and I calmly mutter, "Tonya doesn't have a sister," and she says of course I do and goes on to tell me about her family in Milan and I say, "Tonya's father isn't 52, he's in his sixties," and "Tonya never lived in Brescia, she lived in Trieste," and she says no, no, snap out of it, and we begin to argue and I say this has gone far enough and she says, gently, "I think there's really something wrong with you," and I slam my fist on the table and I shout out this has gone far enough and where the fuck is my girlfriend and everything she's telling me is wrong, wrong, she can't even speak Italian, she says she has dual citizenship, she only speaks English because she grew up in LA and that's wrong wrong wrong, Tonya grew up in Milan and didn't study

English 'till she was 18 and I yell at her who are you and she says Tonya, Jesus Christ, Tonya, and she tells me more details and it's all bullshit it's bullshit it's bullshit it's bullshit

and to make a long story short, we make love, me and this woman, this stranger, and it's nothing like with Tonya and yet it's exactly like with her and she says, we'll figure it out, we'll figure it out, you'll see, and, exhausted, I sleep, breathing easy, breathing, bre

eeping, beeping, beeping, shit, he thinks, shit, he thinks, it's going off, fuck, I knew it, I knew they would call me, it's a Saturday night, a Saturday night, of course they'll need help, sì, sì, sì, don't press, beeping, no, no, not like that, beneath the trousers on the chair, no, no, and he pulls back, stream percolating down his chin to the spreading dark puddle on the mattress, "Th brppr," he says, working his mouth, waking it,

"Cosa?"

"Th beepr," he says, "the beeper," and motions to the muffled wail beneath the sweater the tie the trousers, and she listens, not opening her eyes, confused, a line forms on her brow while he wavers, caressing her burning thigh, and she lets out a gust of breath, rectus abdominus tightening, navel contracting, ah, *merda, vaffanculo, al diavolo quel maledetto cicalino* (loses her English when she's pissed), *lascialo, lascia perdere, che non importa* (her body tense again, her tiny drooping tower of Pisa, who could it be? at 1:30? who?) *quell'aggeggio maledetto, quello stupido cosino* (if not the hospital, who?) *sono sei mesi, sono ben sei mesi che siamo lontani uno dall'atra, sant'Iddio* (the psych section? an eval? no, no way, fuck that) leave it, *non fermarti ora,* leave it, *non è nulla* (she's saying), leave it, please, and looks down at him, between her thighs, her left temple's teensy nevus smirking beneath a curl, unmistakeable in the laughing heater's light, in its pallid, cozy glare, yes, it's still her, and they lock eyes, her big brown puppy eyes, yes, it must be, her eyes say please don't leave me, please don't and part of him wants to cry and he regathers himself, the tinny bawl beneath the trousers now receding, as he goes back on duty, to his pudendal métier, as her head falls back on the pillow and a crooked smile assumes her lips, den, den, den, and one last time he thinks, who? could? it? be? be? be? before launching into the alphabet, the alphabet, the abecedarium she loves, encomius interruptus, his tongue's discourse from its pulpit, its all-night service of letters, letters, letters, save me language, save me, keep her here:

A, B, C, D, E, F, G, H, I, J, (sì, sì, Dio mio) J, J, J, J, J, J, J

esus Christ, what's happening, what's happening, he nearly shrieks, nearly falls out of bed when he sees her, this woman, this naked woman standing before him, caught in the oblong morning window light, as the sleep leaps from his eyes, as she stands there, her back to him, stretching her lean limbs, as she walks to the door, a bronze woman with two moles adorning her scapulae, with hair neither black nor curly nor blonde nor bobbed, a bronze woman with wide hips and narrow shoulders, with straight brown hair that just grazes her coccyx, a beautiful woman whose warmth he can still feel in the sheets, whose earthy smell covers him like a film, who walks, naked, and hears him, who stops, turns, her sensual, shapely lips and wide-set coal-black eyes and thick brows, turns to him with her foreign face and smiles, lovingly — more perfect teeth — and says, in a husky voice, a familiar tone, "Buenos dias," and strides out into the hall, as her steps, her rustles, her words echo through the apartment: "Ay, chingao, now where'd I pack that new conditioner," and the bags are being moved, and I sit up in the bed and the chrome-grilled heater squats smug in the corner and I look all over the pillow and find only long brown hairs, no shoulder-length blonde ones, and the caricature on the wall has a new, darker face … no no no no no, and I jump out of bed and into my robe and she comes back in holding a red plastic bottle, and sees me, my expression, and instantly the smile fades from her lips — though her large brown nipples stay hard in the cold — and she says my name, and what's wrong, and oh, no, not again, and what's wrong and her accent's not American or Italian, and she approaches, approaches, and I back away away away, muttering, mumbling, "What … the … fuck …" and two walls press the sides of my head and she says it's me, it's me, it's Tonya, it's me, and all I can think of is to hit her, hit her, hit her hard across the face, to beat beat beat beat the right face out of her, beat her, it's me, it's Tonya, shut up shut up shut up, beat you, beat you bloody — but no, I don't do that, no, no, I put my fist in my mouth and bite down, and turn away, and before I know it the tears fly from my eyes and the wracks convulse my body, and her arms are around me, tight, and she turns me and sits me and rests my head against her hot, brown breasts, and she rocks me, "Shhhhh, shhhh, silencito, shhh, ya ya," she rocks, and coos, the way Tonya would, and — need I say it? — all the pictures and passports have changed … and that afternoon we're in the city, the museum, she wanted to see the exhibit before it closed, the artist, the Colombian artist that paints fat people and this Tonya (no jet lag), this Tonya (can barely speak English), this Tonya, she wanted to come see it, the exhibit, and I remember the other Tonya — Tonya Tonya — she always liked this guy, this painter, and I never knew why, they're just fat people, I said, there's fat people everywhere, but not like these, she said, these people who look normal in their own little fat universe, their little fatoverse, they're all fat to us but to each other they're normal, normal, ordinary, plain, boring, but to us they're works of art, they're fat but not fat, don't you see? they're different from us but the same as us, *¿entiendes?* and I said, whatever, I said, and felt the sleeping beeper on my belt, and as she walks over to the next picture I realize I'm already used to her thick accent, her bursts of Spanish, they only arouse me more, like the way her jeans hug her ass, that is, gluteus maximus, as she walks, and her history, it no longer matters, I think, they no longer hold weight, these facts, these figures, I've lost count, this Tonya, from Mexico City, she says, six brothers and two sisters and three cats and two degrees, she's never visited LA — and wouldn't want to — her parents married 33 years, six years of study in Guanajuato (la capital), a childhood swimming accident whose details she almost shares with Tonya, my Tonya, Tonya Tonya Tonya, they no longer matter, these details, they puff and smoke and evanesce, like the sterile alcohol smells when he leaves the hospital, because her eyes still light up when they meet his, and her hand still squeezes his pinky as they walk from his car, and his brooch that now says *Te Amo* still dangles from its necklace, bouncing happily between her breasts, and I come up behind her before a big painting of a fat naked woman from Bogotá and turn her by the shoulders and I kiss her, I kiss her long and deep as the fat woman's frame frames us too, as the people walk by us, around us, behind us, before us, trying to see the fat woman but never telling us to move, and back home she turns off the ringer — she knows exactly where the switch is, Tonya's flicked it dozens of times — and I toss my trousers my tie my sweater on the chair and I take her, make love to her like I've never made love to a woman, her body new and her smell different and her taste pristine, but her words, her words are the same: sí, sí, sì, sì, sì, sì, sì, sì, a bit more, così, così, non fermari, così, o, sì, così, sì, sì, *mi fai godere,* she's close, close, nearly there, there, his tongue worn down, half-dead, half-dead, J, J, X, F, Y, HS, OIF, ET, NV, J, J, J, den, den, almost there, almost there, home free, J, J, I, his composition, almost done, their private hypogastric morse code, ode, ode, he writes, she reads, some, one, some, where writes, it, some, one, some, where, peers, it, strangers, al-most-there-home-fr

a click a click a beep a ghostly voice in the reddish dark, they freeze:

honey, I tried beeping you, honey, in case you all were out at dinner or something, but, anyway, did Tonya get in? ¿Como les fue? I thought you were gonna call, call me whenever, okay? bye ... click
     mother,
     mother, Jesus, almost two in the morning, when will she learn, it's later on the
     coast, three years in Hawaii and she still thinks California's earlier, Jesus, Jesus, and the machine rewinds, and the chrome grill keeps laughing, and her rib cage bounces up and down, merda — and then they laugh, laugh, and he kisses her fingers, but she's lost it, she's lost it, her beauty still craves release, he works his coated lips, feels something in his mouth, swallows a hairlet, feel it slither, slither down, a frayed end in their joint tapestry, the clock glows in his periphery, while she, still here, glisters in his sights, and he says I'm sorry, and she breathes out, heavily, no, no, okay, sighing again in mild frustration, as her aching skerry — *ah, prendimi ancora* — her buzzing bothered honeycomb beckons, as she guides his head back down, down, down, dive, dive, dive, dive, though his tongue be half-dead, half-dead, J, J, J, half-dead, J, J
     dead, the woman is dead, DEAD, she lies in my bed as my words catch in mid-sentence, I freeze in the doorway and I see even from there that she's dead, there on my bed, on a Saturday night, with the heater turned off in the corner and the aftershave still in my hand, the caricature fluttering in the open door's draft and my clothes where I threw them on the chair, she's dead, amid all this, all this banality, lying dead, and I dash to her and wince at her coldness, her stiffness, she's dead, her eyes stare at the ceiling glitter, her hands palm up, supine, her breasts in their brownish pallor, dead at

least two hours, two hours (in my professional opinion), but, no, that's impossible, impossible, two hours ago I was inside her, inside this corpse, this cadaver awaiting dissection, no, fuck, I pound her, pound her chest, slap her, scream at her, that's not right, that's not right, and she responds like a mannequin, it's not just dead; the corpse shows no sign that it ever held life, it's wax meat, it's nothing, everything I do to it is nothing, and its burning black eyes seem to swallow, swallow me, swallow the room, and I slap them shut, it keeps staring, straight up, through the lids, motionless, and I see the city lights out the window, and for some reason I get up, bare feet on hardwood, and draw the curtains, and lock the door, and drag the heater over and turn it on, mmmmm, while snails of moisture run down my back, just a shower, I think, I left her alone just long enough to take a shower, but it doesn't matter, not anymore, this naked corpse is all I'm left with, and empty pictures, and fading bags in the hall, and that's it, that's all there is, and I take the towel off from around my waist, and the room is already floating in weak pinkish-red light as I stand there, naked with this morgue prop, this brown carcass-woman, this cold rag doll with whom I spent the day, who I picked up at the airport, who I slept with twice (only once she was a different woman and now she's this one, heh heh), this woman, this woman with whom I pretended, with whom I believed, she lies there revealed, a brown disheveled waste of skin from Mexico, or wherever she was from, lies there dead on arrival, rotting, stinking up the room, and, having nothing better to do, I hate her, hate the bitch, for lying there and leaving me like this, but no, no, the hatred quickly burns out, and I still stand there, how long? and feel a vacuum inside me, no hate, no envy, no regret, nothing, a void, a vacuum, and into this vacuum, completely on its own, seeps the knowledge, the certainty, of what we have to do, yes: we have to operate —

yes, yes, we do, yes we do, gentlemen, and I climb in bed, pull back the sheet, and as I adjust and maneuver, disturbing the mattress, the corpse shifts all as one, in rigor mortis, the stench worsens, riled up, and I get on my knees beside the thing, dispensing with the mask, no, thank you, nurse, and lightly, lightly, I run my lips upon its skin, while my assistants, my colleagues, the clock, the towel, the interning heater, who, tut-tut-tut-ing, all concur with my diagnosis, approve my radical procedure, and so, snapping on their rubber gloves, they prep and drape the patient, while my lips trace the cold linoleum forehead, the alabaster arms, the igneous clavicle, slowly, slowly, slowly, a recon run, on the long, cold, lonely road to hemostasis — turn it over, a gingerbread woman, kiss its cranium, the smooth, foul hair, kiss the vertebrae, sternomastoid, slowly, slowly, trapezius, scapulae with their moles, latissimus dorsi, — over again, please — nose, mouth, throat, pectoralis major, solar plexus, linea alba, slowly, slowly, the countless fault lines beneath the skin, all of it, every inch, kiss it, kiss it, no warmer, no warmer, every orifice smells of rot, slowly, slowly, swallow your sick, still cold, still waiting, slowly, slowly, therapy, move to the cunt? prong? skerry? no, no, not yet, slowly, slowly, obliques, sartorius, rectus femoris, kiss it, kiss it, prepare for incision, prepare to record time, slowly, slowly, ready, doctor, slowly, slowly, the patient, kiss it, the patient's responding, continue treatment, slowly, slowly, don't mind the rot, the patient, keep going, prepare for incision, slowly, slowly, above all don't rush, the patient responding, keep it up, son, keep it up, slowly, slowly, we'll make a surgeon of you yet, by gum, come on, come on, come, come, come

creak, creak, creak, pelvic motions, ultimo stadio, plateau, eau, eau, eau, almost there, ere, ere, ere, she feels the trillion spiders crawl, crawl, crawl, crawl, sucks quick gasps as her body trembles and her little isthmus expands to its full, hard, continental swell, ell, ell, ell, digs her nails into his hair, sì, sì, sì, caro, sì, caro mio, the surf poun-poun-poun-ding, it thunders in her ears — and in his, and in his — she tosses her head left and right, left, right, as his crumbling lingua flashes beyond the pain, won't, stop, won't, stop, J, J, J, J, J, J, J, J, tram, po, line, tram, po, line, keep, on, keep, on, strafe, strafe, strafe, hood, glans, pleasure, beauty, hot, hot, hot, peak, prong,

the mystery, the mystery, she girds herself to go, where he can never follow, ow, ow, ow, ow, he is only the drone, rone, rone, rone, rone, the drone, serving his queen, his queen with clipped wings that only he can restore, ore, the drone who will service her and please her please her please her please her and die once the job is done his tongue on springs, smooth, oiled, up, down, up, down, side, swipe, slip, slide, slip, slideandslipandslide (a breath) andslipandslideandslipandslide won't won't stop

now, now, and the glans, it withdraws, suddenly, now, now, head pressed back mouth wide a growing rumble, ble, ble, ble, and

finally
finally
sì
sì, amore, sì, amore amore, sì
finally
finally

she's there.

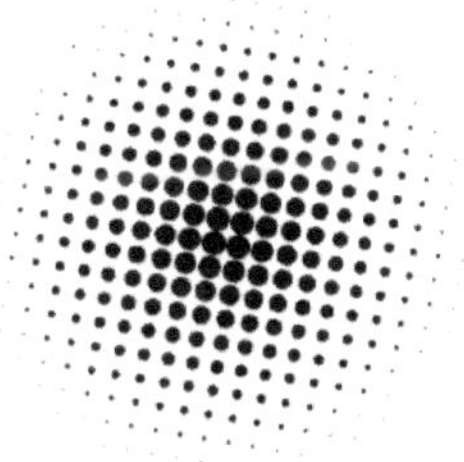

Dad Checks Out

20—

The news of my father's death in Monterrey while on vacation with his family arrived like all such news always seemed to arrive since I started living in Moscow — at 4:30 in the morning.

My mother's crackly voice across the hemispheres broke the story to me quickly, concisely, with the pedestrian cadence of utter normalcy in the face of the extraordinary which I'd long thought peculiar to our family, but which I've since learned exists in many.

Mother, in her matter-of-fact tone, actually spent more time — the larger balance of our $4-a-minute conversation — telling me that an old girlfriend had called after seven years with a sad story of her own, which she'd related, in my absence, to Mom.

I found it strange for Mother to ask if I wanted to know the girl's troubles, since the report of them had originally been intended for me alone, but once I told her to go ahead the tale, in short, went like this: the girl was pregnant from a man she had left, a man she'd been with for a few months following — and this was queer, given my own current circumstances — the death of her perfect husband, whom she'd married seven years before and in the process broken my heart. Now she was back in Texas and unsure what to do, with the baby due in two months and her own mother already dead for six.

All this death jarred me in my Moscow apartment, dusty and unkempt in the bluish light of a slow summer sunrise. Mother said she was on her way to get Father's body, and it was only then that her voice broke, when it seemed all the important information had been related and soon she would have to hang up. My mother hates goodbyes.

I put the receiver back down and returned to my bed, a converted couch in the southwest corner of the city, which I rented from a decrepit pensioner currently, mercifully, away at her dacha for the month.

Lying there under the covers, my balcony window cracked open to what I now considered an appropriately sepulchral though not unpleasant breeze, I immediately thought not of Father, but of the many vivid dreams my sleep had been plying before the phone's apocalyptic ring. They, too — the dreams, I mean — had all had to do with death.

One dream starred an old high school friend, who'd been shot (in the dream, as far as I know not in real life) just above the right lung for some unknown reason. Rumors persisted in school that he had been killed, even after he'd returned to classes looking and acting perfectly normal in his yellow Garanimals shirt, though somehow carrying the aura of the resurrected Lazarus, disoriented, confused, awakened rudely from eternal sleep. In another dream I was pulled over by a cop after what I'd thought was a desperate chase (I'd committed some petty crime before and thought the whole police force was out to run me in), but was in fact an attempt to flag me down so as to inform me of a sad fact: a friend — yet another — had died.

The cop led me, sirens flashing, to the friend's house. Someone was crudely manhandling the body, which belonged — had belonged — to one of the most beautiful and most venal of the many blonde goddesses that populated my college, an empty-headed, full-bodied beauty by the name of Chance. (All this, by the way, was completely made up. I knew no one by that name, though as I said the dead vixen did look somewhat familiar.)

As a crowd gathered outside the girl's perfect upper middle class house, only I seemed to notice what everyone else seemed to miss: she had turned into a man (her own lovely brother, in fact, whom I also "knew"), and he was twitching. He suddenly opened his pretty blue eyes (which a sea of brown eyes, all but my own, failed to detect) and just as quickly shut them up again.

I took it upon myself to revive him. As the crowd (strangely subdued but otherwise behaving not at all abnormally for a dream) stood by, I gave the young man (still named Chance, I assume) the mouth-to-mouth treatment, as well as several other ministrations which must have looked both arcane and well-practiced, but which I had, in fact, learned from an episode of *Star Trek,* the one in which an amnesiac Kirk is stranded on a planet of American Indians and proves to them he's a god by bringing a drowned boy "back to life."

Like Kierok, as he was thenceforth called by the amazed tribe, I delivered my breath to Chance in brief, sharp bursts, massaged his feet and arms to warm them, manipulated various parts of his body, all to astonishingly effective results. He responded to each treatment by opening his eyes, coughing, moving his head, until it was clear that he'd rejoined us in full. The next scene I remember, he was sitting alone on his couch under a sheet in his perfect white living room, I was bringing him some juice. He seemed alive in the physical sense, though not the emotional; he kept staring off into the distance in this sun-drenched (though somehow still shadowed) room and didn't reply when I offered him the glass, as if irritated with me for returning him to the living. So I walked away with loudly echoing steps.

Now I lay in bed, from which all these events had, in fact — in physical fact — sprung, and decided, before dealing with my father, to roll up a prodigious booger — I always have plenty of raw material to work with in the morning — and attempt to dunk it into the shimmeringly distant maw of the wastebasket. I managed to construct a ball about the size of a split pea, and by the sound it made at the end of its trajectory I judged it to have successfully penetrated the basket's air space and settled within, a good left-handed volley.

I suppose it must seem odd — to say the least — to discuss dreams and snot in a story about the death of one's forebears, but, as should be obvious enough by now, Father and I, and for that matter our whole family, had never been especially close. As a child I reacted with horror at this, at first, distressing aspect of our home life, but as with all things, time and habit made it a perfectly normal part of my existence. There has always remained, up to this very day, a painful void within me whenever I thought of our cold familial relations, but the void seemed always muffled, wrapped in the soft cotton, as it were, of long habit, of normalcy, inertia. As long as I could remember, things had been exactly thus, and the few attempts to change this state of affairs only showed, each time more decisively, that thus they would remain. Why try to change the course of the tide? You swim faster, easier, going with it.

Once when I was a teenager we had a demonstration in science class that illustrated the enormity of spatial distances by reducing the solar system to the scale of ordinary human objects. The sun thus became a basketball in the exact center of our town. The earth, the teacher showed, would then be a pea a couple of miles away, at the edge of our small hamlet. Jupiter was a baseball somewhere in the next town, while Pluto, lonely little Pluto, was a cold marble some 15 miles away.

This illustration of the grand scheme of the universe could just as well have represented the dynamics of space between the members of my family, which operated under such distinct and long-established laws as to repel all challenges to its perfect, ordered balance. Mother, father, sister, brother, Kiko the cat, the narrator, all scattered toys across a vast expanse of chilly blackness, catching, as the glint of a distant star permitted, brief reflections of each other across the light years. So it had always seemed to me, and whatever sadness this arrangement carried had long since been borne away on the solar wind of custom.

So the reader might now understand how the catastrophic disappearance of one of those planets — in fact, of the very sun, were we to take the metaphor all the way — had only a minor effect on the orbits of all the other celestial bodies. Our family, normal to the outside world, acted much like some secret conspiracy; the death of a member merely meant the conspiracy would now be reduced by one. Thinned, pared down in number, we would move on.

The gravimetric fluctuation of my father's demise had unbalanced my own orbit, shifted it, forced it to compensate along its dark path, but had not so disoriented as to prevent me from boarding a series of planes that very night from Moscow to New York, New York to Dallas, Dallas to Mexico City and Mexico City to Monterrey, where the day before my father had suffered a massive heart attack in his favorite restaurant's open-air veranda and fallen over onto the cobblestones that had waited 400 years to receive him, along with the spilled contents of his large botana platter: fried shrimp, chicken fajitas, beef fajitas, beans, rice, grilled onions, whole jalapeño peppers, green salsa and the best flour tortillas al norte de la capital. I had once tasted them myself. But if anything, it was the grueling 20-hour trip that had jarred and disoriented me far more than had Father's last convulsions on the stones, though a brief phone conversation with Mother in the Dallas airport did not fail to inject some somberness into my mad itinerary and its mission.

"How does he look?" I had asked. "Not too bad?" After a long silence, my mother's voice broke into tears as she replied, "Yes. He does look very bad, m'ijo."

I judged this to be the opinion of someone who simply hadn't seen my father in a decade and a half and had expected him to look as vital and 44-year-old as the day she had divorced him. My mother and father, never seeing each other, had both stayed in the same town for 15 years after their legal separation, both living with others but never remarrying. My mother, therefore, had been distressed by the man she finally did see upon her arrival in Mexico: older, fatter, more haggard — a distorted reflection, indeed, of how she herself now looked.

Unfortunately, I was wrong, for father did in fact "look very bad, m'ijo." His face was chalky, grossly unnatural in color, his skin the texture of leather and slightly scuffled from his encounter with the stones. He lay in the casket, still looking only as if asleep — familiar people always look only asleep, never really dead, somehow — his expression rather surly, but calm, as if dreaming, as if watching something beneath his eyelids that froze him in place. But, no, he was dead, irrefutably, and no ministrations brought on by Kierok or anyone else would serve to bring him back.

It took only about a minute of this before I burst into tears, tears nourished by Russian viands, incubated in Delta airlines cabins, spilled finally onto my dead father's cuff deep inside the Mexico he had loved, the motherland we had all lost long, long ago. I turned to my little half brothers and their mother, the woman with whom my father had lived for almost ten years. I ran my hand briefly, fondly, through the little boys' jet black hair; that was somehow all I ever seemed to do with them, the only contact we ever shared. They were just some more tiny planets from an even more distant galaxy, but still I could see my father, bold and blatant, staring back at me from their watery black eyes. A few more minutes, silent and thoughtful, were all that seemed necessary. My mother and I then walked arm-in-arm to our hotel to rest for the long trip home.

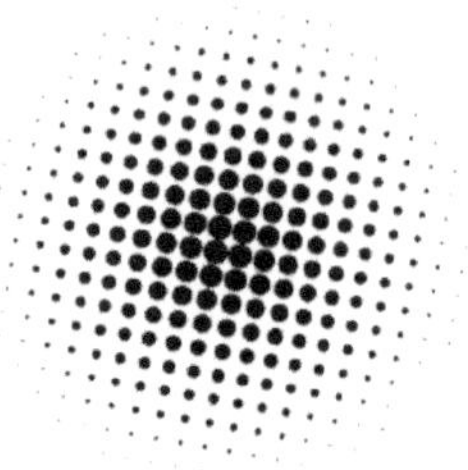

Where You Stop the Story

1984/2022

— want to try to write some of this down. So let me just go through it. So, it's 1982. I'm 14 years old. I'm with my grandfather, my grandmother and my father, on our way to Florida. We're driving it all the way. 24 hours.

No, my parents were still together. They didn't divorce until '84. My mother didn't go I guess because this was something on the Alaniz side of the family, and she didn't care for long drives in a crowded car. I think so, anyway. I don't know; all the people I could ask have now died or have dementia. I don't know. Anyway, it was four of us in the car. My grandpa and Dad both had experience with long-haul driving, they could drive for fucking ever. They just wanted to do it all the way straight, alternating between the two of them. No hotel, no nothing. So we just drove all the way through from the Valley to Florida.

Another thing: this happened in Winter. That's important later. So, yeah, we had no problems getting to Florida. I only remember they picked me up at school and off we went. I have no memory of crossing those states in between. Then when we got to Florida, we stopped to get gas or eat or something. I remember crisp, chilly morning air. The light looked different from Texas somehow. There was an older man outside the restaurant or whatever, sitting there, wearing a beret, maybe? Or a tweed cap? He was talking, maybe smoking a cigarette. I don't remember what he said, but it was how he spoke that totally stopped me in my tracks. He was speaking Spanish with a Cuban accent. I had never heard that before. Fourteen years old, and I had never heard that. He spoke fast too, faster than us. It just felt like it opened up a whole new view on the world, you know, like, that people spoke Spanish in different ways. That our Spanish was just one way. One of many. Travel's so damn important for that. I tried fried bananas for the first time too…

Okay, so everything depends on where you stop the story. I could stop it right here, with a nice moral about the value of travel or whatever. But let's go on.

So I'm 14 years old in 1982 and I'm in Florida with my grandfather and my grandmother and my father. Let me tell you that story. … sorry, what?

It was for a wedding. Okay. Yeah. And so we were — actually, it's not bad if you ask me questions.

What city? Uh, Gainesville area, maybe? It was in the boonies. I forget exactly where. But, anyway, so we go to the wedding. And so this was the only time I met a lot of those people. A lot of 'em have died. Great-aunts, second cousins, third cousins. And I was 14 years old, and we're at the reception and that was the first time I ever got drunk. I had something to drink, probably beer, but I was a kid, it didn't take much. So I'm dancing, and I fell, just stumbling around. There was a hot girl my age, I remember, too. So I really impressed her. So that was funny. People saw me falling, they laughed. Even years later, that's the part everybody remembered. My dad and grandma would bring it up, grinning: "Remember when you got drunk and fell at the reception, mi'jo?" I guess that's the one image all those strangers will ever have of me.

So, funny story, could end it right there. A trip, a wedding, family, boy coming of age, overdoes the booze and embarasses himself. Done.

But let's keep going. So then, after the reception and all of that, and, you know, just getting to meet everybody, and, uh … Oh, you know what? … Did that happen then …? I think it did. Yeah, it must have. I only ever took that one trip to Florida. It's weird, because I was kinda young for it … But, well, after the wedding, I mean like the next day or something, one of my cousins who was older than me by a considerable amount — because he was, or he must have been, like an adult already — well, he took me to a strip club. Or at least some place in Florida, like a bar, that happened to have naked women.

I just remember a stripper, topless, giving a lap dance to a pretty, like, *Deliverance*-looking guy with a long beard. Like a lumberjack. Huh? A scruffy guy, right. And she was doing it to *Sea of Love,* sung by Robert Plant and the Honeydrippers. That was a song that was around at that time. Yeah, I'm trying to … or maybe I'm conflating two different memories. Probably so, because I remember another strip club — they're all dark, they all look the same — in San Diego where they had Scope mouthwash and shit next to the couches and armchairs where they did the lap dances, 'cause the customers' breath stank, I guess. That was a lot like this place in Florida, but, no, it wasn't the same. Hold on …

But still, all this seems strange, because, like, why would they have let in a 14-year old? Did my cousin know the bouncer or something …?

Oh, shit. It must have been 1984.

Wikipedia tells me that *Sea of Love* didn't come out until November of '84. That must have been it. It was 1984 and I was 16. Yeah, I guess that *is* right. When they picked me up, it was from the high school …

So this *did* happen after my parents had separated and were in the middle of the divorce. Shit, so now there's, like, a whole political dimension here that I forgot about. How did this trip figure in that, I wonder? I mean, my grandparents, que en paz descansen, they treated my mother pretty rough during the divorce, trying to wrest the house from her, and my father went along. Bien gachos, como dicen. Dad was a little slow with my child support, too, Mom always said …

Hmmm … I seem to recall asking my mother if I could go on this trip, and her having no problem with it. But was she just putting on a brave face? Did she feel like I was turning my back on her by going to this Alaniz thing in Florida? (She definitely felt that way later about me spending time with Dad …) Was Dad just trying to play nice to get out of some child support payments? Who knows …

So, whatever. That makes a lot more sense. I would have been 16 years old, not 14, and wouldn't've stood out as much in some sleazy strip joint. So I guess I didn't have my first beer 'til 16. And that was my first strip club. I sure picked up some vices in Florida …

So, anyway, I could stop here. A story about the flimsiness of memory, family trauma, a boy becoming a man, que la chinga … But no.

It's really the ride home, after the wedding and everything, that I want to talk about.

So, to back up a little bit. Even before we left Texas, I had begged my

Dad to go to Disney World in Florida. That might have been the main attraction of the trip for me, in fact. So, after the family thing, we went. Now, we had gone to Disney*land* in 1977, in California, as a family: Mom, Dad, my sister and brother and I. That was my first time on a plane. I was much younger then, of course. Nine. But, now, in Florida, this was different. I was 16, but still enough of a kid that I wanted to go. But now that I know this happened while the divorce was going on … Did my father maybe want to go to Disney World too, to relive happier times, family times, good old times? Was that the determining factor? I seem to recall Grandpa not wanting to make the trip to Orlando, which would take us out of the way and of course cost a shitload in tickets for four people. (I remember we also drove through Tampa Bay, but that's not relevant.) But maybe Dad and I insisted …

Anyway, we went.

And it really was magical.

I mean, I saw the Alanizes behave in ways I had never seen before and never saw again. And they all lived another 30-40 years! Because they were laughing, they were like little kids. Riding the rides, seeing the sights. I saw my grandfather and grandmother walking *hand in hand* down Main Street, USA. I had never seen them hold hands. I don't think I ever saw them kiss. Yeah, but they were holding hands and smiling and laughing like they were on a first date or something. Like with the Cuban man speaking Spanish, it was like a whole new world or alternate universe or something opened up right in front of me. Jaw-dropping stuff.

And my Dad. He just wandered off on his own. I guess he was supposed to be watching me, but Dad was not what you might call attentive in these situations …

Right. He was not a "helicopter parent." I told you about that time he lost me in Mexico when I was four or five. But anyway, I was 16 now. It was no big deal. So Dad went off somewhere. He probably told me to just go do whatever. I'm a lot like him that way. So I remember he just went to go do his thing, no plan to meet up again or anything. But it was okay. Disney World is not the streets of Reynosa, and 16 is not four. It was fine.

Yeah. Anyway, so before I know it I see my father in the distance, coming out of a magic shop. He sees me and smiles, walks up, shows me the goodies in his bag. He had bought all this magic crap, little trick cards and exploding cigars or whatever. He was like a child, his face all lit up with his treasures, like me with comic books. So again, that just opened up a whole side of my father that you'd hardly ever see and that actually I recognize in myself because I buy all kinds of crap like that. And I do it to this day — and I'm ten years older now than he was then in 1984 in Disney World, Florida, USA!

So yeah, that's it. It's a very happy memory. We did the rides, had cotton candy, saw the cuetes over the castle, etc. etc. And like I said, it was just a really rare circumstance. Unique. But then, in just a few hours, all that ended up getting shat on. Because on the ride back home, my father and grandfather did all the driving again, and they were just set on going all the way straight through, 24 hours like before. All the way to Edinburg.

But now there'd been a cold front. An ice storm. And the roads really were slick. Pero eran tercos los dos, they didn't want to stop anywhere. Maybe we were low on money after Disney World, we couldn't afford a hotel? I doubt it. But who knows — a lot of shit goes over your head, even at 16. I kept my mouth shut.

But my grandmother. Damn, that was sad. My grandmother kept, like, telling them that she was all worried, she thought we were going to die. And it's true, we were going over iced bridges, skidding on the road in the middle of the night who knows where, slipping and sliding. Snow swirling everywhere. But they didn't give a fuck, they just kept going. Especially Grandpa, he didn't want to slow down, he wanted to get home, like it was a race or something. (Did he have some pressing business?)

And Grandma was just pleading and begging from the back seat that we stop, we were going to die. And, yes, she could be very dramatic, very ansiosa. And yes, she could exaggerate and overreact to things. But this weather was no joke … So, it goes on like that for hours: Dad and Grandpa, probably more nervous than they're letting on, driving through the night in a winter storm, skidding here and there, and Grandma begging diosito Jesús not to let us die. Loud.

Sure, she was a little over the top, a little too emotional, wailing and shit. But she was terrified.

And then finally, my Grandfather just snaps and yells at her from the passenger seat, "Ya cállate, mujer, cállate Chona!" The cab filled up with his roar, shook with it. I see his enraged face, all Hulked up in a rictus, sweat beading his brow. Damn, did he even say, "Cállate lo sico"? That would have been bad — a real breach. Did he go so far as to raise his hand to her, and she winced, pressed back against her seat? That part's fuzzy. I might be imagining that. I hope so. The real thing was bad enough. In short, all that good will from Disney World a few paragraphs back, that all just evaporated.

So, she quieted down after that. But she kept praying, mumbling, crying to herself in her corner of the car. Light from streetlights or whatever would sometimes fall on her face, a portrait of despair. Now she only had me to complain to, since I was riding in the back with her. She would turn to me and tell me things, softly. She said, you know, we have to pray to God, we have to pray to God to save us.

And then, after a lot of that, she stops and stares. She looks at me close in the dark, like she's never really seen me before, and says, "Tú no crees en Dios, verdad?"

Well, what could I say? "Pues, no, granmá."

It was the wrong thing, of course. I should have just lied: "Sí, creo en El. Sí, con todo mi corazon. Sí, creo en El y lo quiero mucho. Lo quiero a El y a su hijo y a su chingada madre, granmá." Yeah, that phrasing could maybe use another draft.

But see, I guess in my 16-year-old brain I felt like, in her hour of profound darkness, I at least owed my grandmother my honesty. Which just shows you how fucked up my 16-year-old brain was. In moments of real terror and despair, people don't want honesty. I wish that now, in middle age, I could tell you that I've learned that lesson well, but ...

So anyway, Grandma thought we were all gonna freeze to death and on top of that her unbeliever grandson's soul was gonna burn in eternal hellfire (or whatever). I don't know. I don't know what she was thinking, exactly. You never really know. I mean, how Catholic was she, de veras? This very superstitious woman who had done the ojo curanderismo thing on me with the egg when I was a wee lad? Not exactly Vatican-approved. And the way she treated my mother after the divorce ... Ah, let's move on.

So yeah, it was just a really desperate time for my grandmother in the back seat, thinking for hours that she's gonna die on these horrible iced roads, and maybe they weren't even that bad. I couldn't judge. You know, I could tell that they were icy and I could feel that we were skating a little bit, but then again Grandpa and Dad had a lot more experience as drivers, and they said they could manage. If anything, yeah, I probably thought Grandma was taking things too far, like she always did. But it was still just such a time of sadness for her; she felt terribly worried about her family and she couldn't do anything about it. She was in hell. So what if she was exaggerating? (The macho gender power dynamics of the scene have not escaped me either.) All I could do was say over and over that things would be alright, don't worry.

And so it went until we dipped out of the ice, southward, and sailed on. We made it back, obviously. And that was our Florida adventure.

But what I wanted to do with this piece, and I hope I can write it, is I wanted to talk about how it works as a template, an example — or maybe I should just say a critique — of storytelling. Because everything depends on where you stop.

Like I said, I could stop the story so that it's about, oh, you know, a nice wedding trip. I got drunk and fell and everybody laughed. Ha ha.

Or I could go on and tell about how then we went to Disney World. And everybody was so happy. Everything was just great, beautiful, perfect. I could end it with my grandfather and grandmother holding hands, walking off down Main Street USA to go get some pinche cotton candy. Colorín colorado, chúpenmela pendejos.

Or I could keep going, and then it turns into a horrible shitshow: iced roads, slough of despond, verbal abuse, crisis of faith, generational betrayal y la chinga.

It all depends on where you stop the story. But on the other hand, as it happens, the story did end, sort of. Naturally, you might say, and on a banal key. We made it back home, like Odysseus. What I mean is that, for all his fantastic exploits, Odysseus does finally make it back to Ithaca,[6] and getting home is the most banal of all actions in a narrative — with the exception of the beginning, I guess. Getting back home safe is usually what signals the end of the story. We didn't get killed, we made it.

But then, you know, why stop there? I could keep going and say that my parents finalized their divorce, my father remarried, I got some new brothers … We're going right here. It's right, yeah. You stay on the 3 north

---

[6]Yes, I know that at home Odysseus still has to vanquish Penelope's suitors; you know what I mean, no chinges.

for the next 7.3 miles. So, yeah, the whole of the trip — "there and back again" — is a kind of vessel for the story. But a leaky vessel, leaky as hell. That's why I picked this event, because it seems like the usual container for a story (beginning, middle, end), but now I could go on to tell you about years later and my father's cancer; my grandmothers' dialysis torture; me cutting some hair from Grandpa's corpse for safekeeping; Mom's dementia; finding new branches of our family that Grandpa had kept hidden, things like that — or years before, like my father's complicated relationship since childhood with Grandpa; Grandpa's own abandonment issues (as a child his mother left him); Granmá's trauma as an émigré to the States during the Mexican Revolution (she was just a baby); the fact that my mother already knew a lot of those people in Florida, having met them long before, and so on. Those threads (crucial, incidental) all stretch forward and backward in time through that Florida event, complicating and adding layers to everyone's behavior over those few days. And we don't even need to stop with their deaths: stuff Grandpa did and didn't do, for example, continues to affect our lives today. Things are still happening.

And what about me, you may ask? No shit; I'm the one telling you all this — and more importantly, choosing how to tell it.

I guess what I mean is there is no story. And if there is no story, no *one* story, then there's no one ending either. To put an ending to a story is really too scary of a power; I kinda wish I didn't have it. It assigns a false and artificial meaning to a tale, and when the tale's based on life it oversimplifies real, complex, inscrutable people (to say nothing of other beings). But then, stories themselves are artificial, oversimple constructs, aren't they?

So, you want to stop this one now? Yeah?

Okay, the end.

By the way, I —

ELECTRIC YOUTH

A cartoon compendium by José Alaniz

BZZZZ!

I ALWAYS CONSIDERED IT A DEFINING MOMENT IN MY HISTORY. I MUST'VE BEEN THREE OR FOUR. I WAS TRYING TO TURN OFF AN AC WALL UNIT, AND HADN'T MASTERED THE CONCEPT OF KNOBS. BUT I PULLED AT THE PLUG CORD AND GOT AN INCREDIBLE FEELING, LIKE A MILLION TINY HANDS ALL PULLING ME AT ONCE. INDESCRIBABLE.

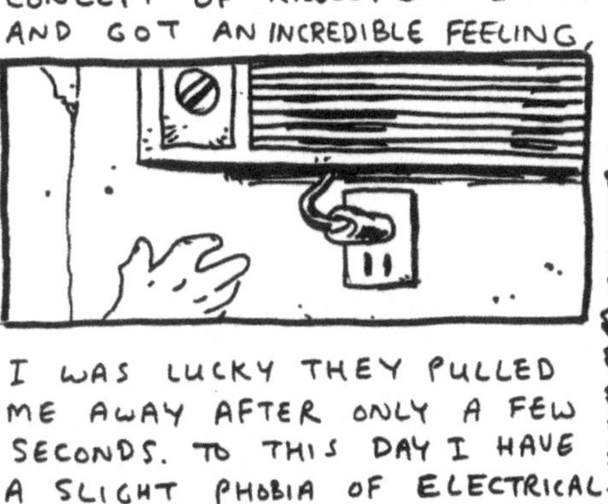

I WAS LUCKY THEY PULLED ME AWAY AFTER ONLY A FEW SECONDS. TO THIS DAY I HAVE A SLIGHT PHOBIA OF ELECTRICAL OUTLETS. SHOCKING, HUH?

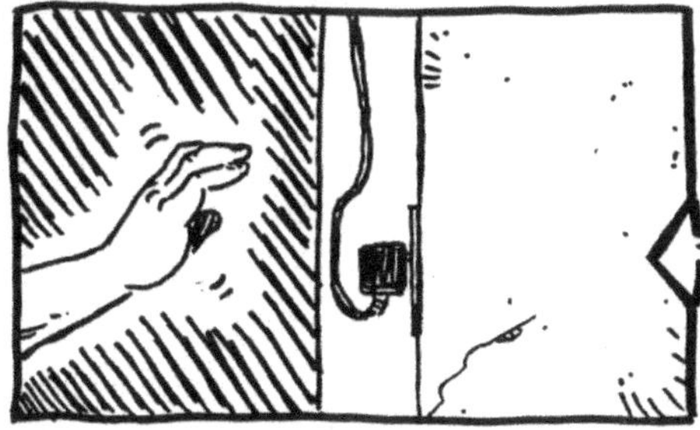

FRAGMENTS

ONE OF MY EARLIEST MEMORIES IS OF CLIMBING UP ONTO THE SCREEN AREA AT THE MOVIES. PEOPLE YELLED AND WE GOT IN TROUBLE, BUT I DISCOVERED TO MY AMAZEMENT THAT THE FIGURES ON THE SCREEN WERE NOT REAL, BECAUSE I COULDN'T TOUCH THEM.

I VAGUELY RECALL SEEING NIXON ON TV AT MY GRANDMOTHER'S. THIS MIGHT HAVE BEEN WHEN HE RESIGNED.

I REMEMBER ON A FLIGHT TO MICHIGAN THERE WAS A SPIDER CLINGING TO THE OUTSIDE OF THE AIRPLANE WINDOW. IT HUNG ON, EVEN AFTER WE WERE IN THE AIR, SOMEHOW.

BUT MY EARLIEST MEMORY, IF THAT'S WHAT IT IS, IS SEEING THE LIGHTS OF DALLAS GLOWING LIKE STARS IN THE NIGHT. WE MOVED TO DALLAS SHORTLY AFTER I WAS BORN.

FRAGMENTS II

MORE EARLY BITS AND PIECES. A SMALL FROG HOPPING ABOUT AS MY DAD WATERED THE SEEDS IN OUR BRAND-NEW BACK YARD, STILL EARTHEN. AROUND THEN A BIG CEMENT MIXER POURED OUT THE CONCRETE PATHS ...

GRANDMA' CONCHA'S LEMON GRASS TE' CON LECHE, HARVESTED FROM HER GARDEN. TO THIS DAY I CAN'T SMELL IT WITHOUT THINK-ING OF HER ...

THE NIGHT THE BODEGA ABOUT A BLOCK FROM US BURNED DOWN. THE RAILROAD TRACKS NEXT TO OUR HOUSE LED RIGHT UP TO IT.

JENNIFER'S FACE.

EL OTRO LADO

MEXICO WAS 20 MILES AWAY. WE'D GO THERE A LOT, FOR DIFFERENT THINGS. MY MOM KNEW A TAROT WOMAN THERE WHO'D READ HER FORTUNE EVERY OTHER MONDAY EXCEPT HOLIDAYS.

MY DAD AND BROTHER AND I WENT FOR HAIRCUTS. ONCE I GOT SEPARATED FROM DAD IN A CROWD AND CRIED. I SOON FOUND HIS FACE IN THE THRONG, VERY CALM. HE SAID HE KNEW I COULD CARE FOR MYSELF.

MY SISTER LOVED THE SHOPPING. SHE LIKED THE MERCADO, WITH ALL ITS COLORFUL DRESSES AND TRINKETS. I WAS MORE FASCINATED BY THE BEGGARS.

AND WE ALL LOVED THE FOOD. MY FAVORITE WAS CABRITO, OR GOAT MEAT. I LOVED CABEZITA (GOAT'S HEAD). THE BRAINS AND ESPECIALLY THE EYES WERE DELICIOUS, PROBABLY BECAUSE THEY WERE SO DIFFERENT.

ALONE

MY DAD HAD DROPPED ME OFF AT MY GRANDPARENTS' HOUSE, BUT THEY WERE OUT. I'D NEVER BEEN ALONE BEFORE. WHAT COULD I DO?

THE TOYS IN MY BOX COULDN'T HELP ME. THEY STARED UP, DEFENSELESS. I WAS GETTING SCARED.

AT LAST I DECIDED TO BE BRAVE AND TRY TO WALK BACK HOME. I INSTINCTIVELY KNEW IT WASN'T TOO FAR AWAY, BUT I'D NEVER REALLY PAID ATTENTION HOW TO GET TO PLACES. AND THE WORLD WAS SO **HUGE**. MY TOYS RATTLED.

I WALKED BACK TO GRANDMA AND GRANPA'S, CRYING. WHEN THEY FINALLY GOT BACK, GRANDMA SAID MY FACE LOOKED STREAKED. I DIDN'T ADMIT THE REASON.

ELECTRIC YOUTH
MORDIDO
ONCE AS A KID I GOT CHASED BY A DOG. I RAN SO FAST I LOST MY SHOES. HE GOT ME IN THE LEG ANYWAY. BUT THE REAL LESSON CAME WITH WHAT HAPPENED NEXT...
MY MOTHER'S REACTION.
IT DOESN'T LOOK SO BAD. PUT SOME NEOSPORIN ON IT.
MY GRAND-MOTHER'S REACTION.
¡AY DIOSITO! ¡VÁMONOS AL HOSPITAL!

I GOT A RABIES SHOT. THEN SHE MADE ME TAKE HER TO WHERE IT HAPPENED. THERE SHE YELLED AT THE OWNERS. AS LUCK HAD IT, THEY WERE THE ONLY ANGLOS ON THE BLOCK. I HAD TO TRANSLATE MY GRAND-MOTHER'S ANGRY TIRADE AND HIS ANSWERS BACK AND FORTH. HUMILIATING. AND IT TAUGHT ME A REAL LESSON ABOUT MY PLACE IN THE WORLD...
¡!
!!
ALL FRIENDLY NOW
I GOT BIT.
ME MORDIERON.

ELECTRIC YOUTH
UNA CUCHARITA de Azúcar
QUIERO AGRADECER A LA SUERTE QUE TUVE ESE DÍA CUANDO DE NIÑO CASI ME MACHUCÓ UN CARRO. SUBÍ MIS BRAZOS PARA DETENERLO, Y ME SENTÍ COMO UN SUPERHÉROE. DESPUÉS MI MAMÁ ME DIO UNA CUCHARITA DE AZÚCAR PARA EL SUSTO. ¡PERO YO NI LO TENÍA!

Quiero dar gracias por la buena fortuna que tuvo mi familia cuando se hizo un fuego dentro de nuestro garaje. Mi hermano Pedro perdió todo el pelo de su cabeza, pero no murió, porque mi papa le hechaba agua de la manguera y corrió pa fuera. Nuestra casa no se quemó. Por eso doy gracias.

EL OJO

ONCE I HAD THE FLU OR SOMETHING AND MY GRAND-MOTHER DECIDED TO CURE ME OF "EL OJO" – THE EVIL EYE.

SHE TOOK AN EGG AND RUBBED IT ALL OVER MY BODY, AND PRAYED. THE EGG FELT COLD AND FUNNY. THE EVIL SPIRIT CAUSING MY FLU WAS SUPPOSED TO BE ABSORBED INTO THE EGG.

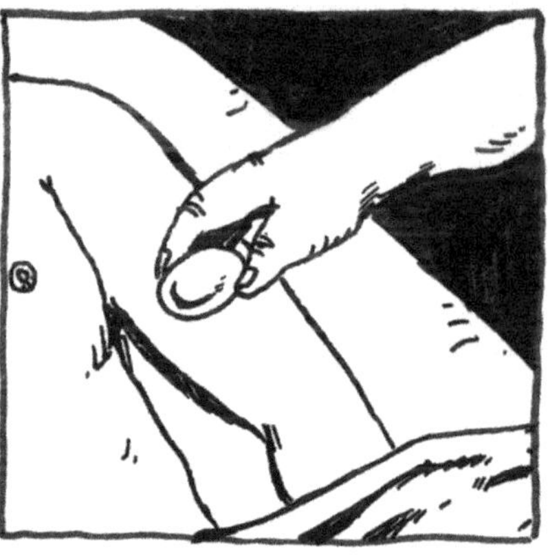

THEN SHE CRACKED THE EGG AND PUT THE YOLK INTO A GLASS OF WATER. THIS RELEASED THE EVIL SPIRIT TO FLY AWAY INTO THE AIR.

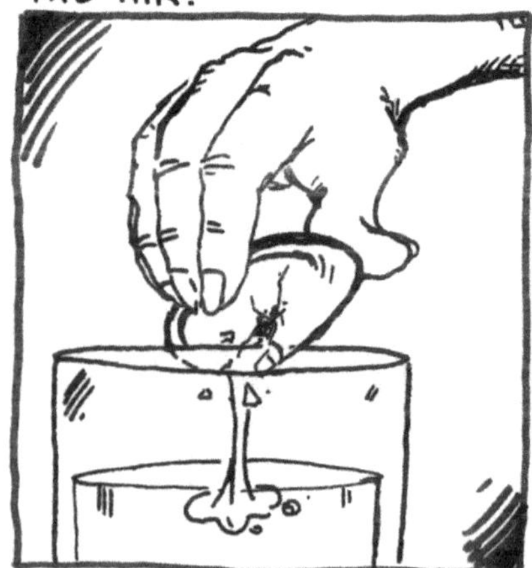

FOR SOME REASON, YOU WERE ALWAYS SUPPOSED TO LEAVE THE YOLK UNDER YOUR BED OVERNIGHT. I THINK I GOT BETTER SOON AFTER, BUT IF THIS WAS BECAUSE "EL OJO" WAS GONE, I DON'T KNOW.

SCARY

AS A KID GROWING UP IN THE VALLEY, MY RELATIVES AND FRIENDS WOULD ALWAYS FILL MY HEAD WITH "STORIES THAT MUST NOT DIE"— GHOST STORIES AND OTHER SCARY MEXICAN FOLK TALES.

THERE WAS "EL CUCÚY," OR BOGEYMAN, WHO WOULD COME IN THE NIGHT AND EAT YOU IF YOU DIDN'T BEHAVE. "AY VIENE EL CUCÚY!" MY DAD WOULD ALWAYS SAY, "HERE COMES CUCÚY!"

AND "LA LLORONA," OR "WEEPING WOMAN," A GHOSTLY MOTHER WHO WEPT FOREVER FOR HER DROWNED BABIES. MY SISTER HAD ME CONVINCED THAT LA LLORONA LIVED IN THIS ALLEY NEAR OUR HOUSE, AND I WAS TERRIFIED TO WALK BY IT AT NIGHT.

THEN THERE WAS "LA LECHUSA," ALSO KNOWN AS "BIG BIRD." IT WOULD SWOOP OUT OF THE SKY AND PLUCK COWS RIGHT OFF THE FIELDS AND EAT THEM. LA LECHUSA WAS EVEN REPORTED ON THE LOCAL EVENING NEWS. I ALWAYS IMAGINED IT AS SORT OF A GIANT PELICAN.

FRUITFUL

THOUGH THEY WERE OUR LIVELIHOOD, I RARELY WENT OUT TO HARVEST SANDIAS(WATERMELONS). WHEN I DID GO TO THE FIELDS, I'D SIT IN THE AIR-CONDITIONED OFFICE WITH MY SISTER AND COMPETE WITH THE FLY PAPER TO SEE WHO COULD KILL MORE MOSCAS (FLIES).

OUTSIDE, IN THE HOT SUN, THE MIGRANT WORKERS GATHERED THE SANDIAS, TOSSING THEM ALONG THE LINE TO BE STACKED IN TRUCKS. I SOMETIMES HELPED BY WIPING OFF DUST AND DEAD WORMS. THE WORKERS CALLED ME "GUERITO"— "THE LITTLE WHITE ONE." THEIR CONTEMPT UPSET ME.

ONCE MY SISTER WAS DRIVING ME HOME FROM THE FIELDS AND SHE FELT REAL SICK. SHE SAID SHE HAD THESE PAINS THAT ONLY GIRLS GET, WHICH I FOUND HARD TO BELIEVE. WHY SHOULD ONLY GIRLS GET THEM?

WE STOPPED AT A GAS STATION. MY SISTER WENT IN AND I WAITED. I FELT SORRY FOR HER, BUT I STILL DIDN'T UNDERSTAND. WAS SHE PREGNANT? THOUGH I ALSO DIDN'T QUITE KNOW WHAT THAT MEANT, EITHER.

ONE TIME 'N KINDERGARTEN

BECAUSE I WOULDN'T OWN UP TO IT, AND IT REEKED SO BAD, THE TEACHER MADE US GO TO THE BATHROOM, WHERE SHE CHECKED US, ONE BY ONE.

I GOT SENT HOME, AND SAT IN THE PLASTIC POOL...*

*MY GRANDMOTHER TOLD ME TO FILL IT WITH SOME WATER AND SIT IN IT IN MY UNDERWEAR, ¡ME CAGUÉ!

BROWNIE
WE HAD A PUPPY ONLY ONCE IN OUR FAMILY. THE DAY WE GOT HIM, ME AND MY BIG SISTER NAMED HIM BROWNIE.
ON THE WAY HOME, WE SAT IN THE BED OF GRANDPA'S TRUCK. BROWNIE...
...GOT SCARED AND JUMPED OUT ONTO THE HIGHWAY.
MY SISTER JUMPED AFTER HIM, AND MY GRANDFATHER ACCIDENTALLY RAN OVER HER LEG AS HE WAS BACKING UP FOR US.
SHE SCREAMED A LONG TIME AT THE HOSPITAL.
BROWNIE WAS KILLED ON THE HIGHWAY. WE NEVER HAD A PUPPY AGAIN.
HAZY MEMORY = GENERIC DOG

BURNING BASKET

WE WERE PLAYING
WITH MATCHES.
I WAS 10 OR 11.
I KEPT TOSSING
THEM INTO THE
WASTE BASKET FULL
OF TISSUE PAPER, TO
SEE IF IT WOULD
CATCH FIRE.

SUDDENLY, THE FLAMES FLARE UP DRAMATICALLY — AND I BOLTED OUT OF THE ROOM. I LOOKED BACK, TERRIFIED, AND THOUGHT I SAW SPARKS RAINING DOWN ONTO OUR SHAG RUG, LIKE A ROMAN CANDLE. THAT DAY I SHOCKED MYSELF WITH MY CAPACITY FOR COWARDICE.

BANANA BIKE
A TRAGEDY
REAL PIC. REAL SHIRT.
I LOVED THAT BIKE! BEST BIKE I EVER HAD!
THEN THIS HAPPENS...
I'M RIDING OUT BY APOLLO PARK. MINDING MY OWN BEE'S WAX. SOME MEAN KIDS ON THEIR OWN BIKES START CHASING ME. DON'T KNOW WHY. ONE OF THEM, AS WE'RE PEDALING, GRABS MY "SISSY BAR" AND...
I LIMPED HOME. WHAT COULD I DO? NO MORE BANANA BIKE.

OH NO!
ONCE, AS A DUMB KID I DROPPED A BAG OF GOLDFISH!
"THE FISHIES!"
I SCREAMED. FORTUNATELY THEY LIVED, IN THE TINY POCKET OF WATER LEFT, ALL THE WAY HOME.

THE NAIL

ONCE AT MY AUNT'S HOUSE I STEPPED ON A RUSTY NAIL. IT DIDN'T GO THROUGH ALL THE WAY.

THE FUNNY THING WAS, I TOLD MY DAD AND HE SAID THE SAME THING HAD HAPPENED TO HIM AS A BOY. ONLY HIS NAIL WENT ALL THE WAY THROUGH, AND HAD WOOD ATTACHED TO IT.

THEY TOOK ME TO THE HOSPITAL, AND THE EMERGENCY ROOM NURSE SAID I STUNK LIKE A SKUNK AS SHE GAVE ME A TETANUS SHOT. I'D BEEN OUT PLAYING ALL DAY.

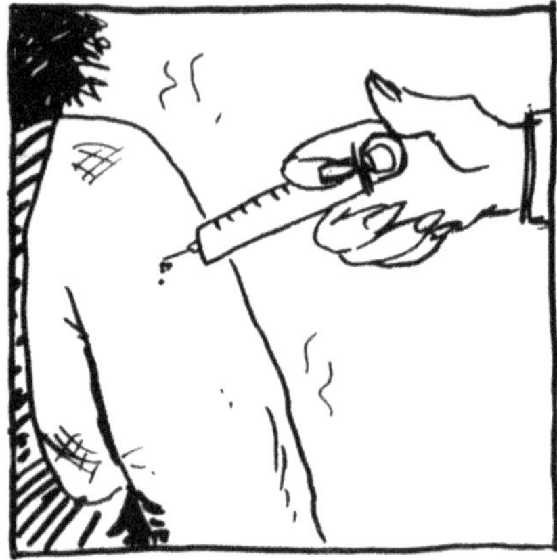

A STRANGER CAME AND CARRIED HIM. WITH EVERY STEP, THE WOOD PLANK WOULD SHIFT, AND HURT LIKE HELL, MY DAD SAID.

THE TRUNK
IT WAS JUST A TRUNK, TACKY,
COLORED, VINYL LI-NING, WHERE I KEPT MY TOYS. IN MY CLOSET. I OPEN IT, LIKE A THOUSAND TIMES BEFORE ...
MULTI-SOMETHING I CAN'T SEE AND CAN'T UNSEE SHRIEKS AT ME, GROWLS, SLASHES AT ME WITH ITS CLAWS. THEN IT'S GONE, LIKE IT NEVER EXISTED.
WHAT WAS IT? "WAS" IT??
I ONLY KNOW: IT WAS IN THE TRUNK.

Not proud of this one.

As a kid I went through a phase when I hated Mexicans. Pretty dumb, since the Valley is, like, 90% Mexican — including me. At the mall, I would imagine the many brown bodies coming at me as imperial T.I.E. fighters for me to shoot down. Pathetic.

DRIVING DOWN MONTE CRISTO IN EDINBURG TODAY, I REMEMBER A DIFFERENT NIGHT ON THIS ROAD, LONG AGO, IN ANOTHER CAR.

HIGH SCHOOL. I'M BROKEN-HEARTED OVER A GIRL. I'M LISTENING TO ZEPPELIN'S "SINCE I'VE BEEN LOVING YOU" ON CASSETTE. LOUD.

TEARS STREAMING, I FLOOR IT TO COAST RIGHT UP BEHIND A SEMI GOING 60mph. "IF IT SUDDENLY BRAKES," I'M THINKING, "I'M DEAD." "IT'S NOT SUICIDE, RIGHT? IF SOMEBODY ELSE STOPPING MAKES ME CRASH?" "IT'S OUT OF MY HANDS."

AFTER ABOUT A MILE AT HIGH SPEED, BUMPER TO BUMPER BEHIND AN 18-WHEELER, ABOUT AS STUPID AS STUPID GETS —
THE SPELL BROKE.

I TOLD NO ONE.

Puro Pinche Author Bio

Born and raised in Edinburg, TX, **José Alaniz** has worn a few hats over the years, including those of journalist, cartoonist and spinner of yarns. His work has appeared in *The Bobcat News Journal*, *The Daily Texan*, *Analecta*, *The Moscow Tribune*, *The Berkeley Fiction Review*, *The Mesquite Review*, *The Stranger*, the Seattle anthology *Dune*, *AltCom: How To Survive a Dictatorship* (2018), *Tales From La Vida: A Latinx Comics Anthology* (2018), *BorderX: A Crisis in Graphic Detail* (2020) and *SCARFFF*. He is also a professor in the Department of Slavic Languages and Literatures and the Department of Cinema & Media Studies (adjunct) at the University of Washington, Seattle. He has published three monographs: *Komiks: Comic Art in Russia* (University Press of Mississippi, 2010); *Death, Disability and the Superhero: The Silver Age and Beyond* (UPM, 2014); and *Resurrection: Comics in Post-Soviet Russia* (OSU Press, 2022). He has also co-edited two essay collections, *Comics of the New Europe: Reflections and Intersections* (with Martha Kuhlman, Leuven University Press, 2020) and *Uncanny Bodies: Disability and Superhero Comics* (with Scott T. Smith, Penn State University Press, 2019). He formerly chaired the Executive Committee of the International Comic Arts Forum (ICAF) and was a founding board member of the Comics Studies Society. In 2020 he published his first comics collection, *The Phantom Zone and Other Stories* and in 2023 his second, *The Compleat Moscow Calling* (both from Amatl Comix). He lives blissfully in rural Washington state with his wife and many animals.